Stand-off at Copper Town

When Nathan Palmer and Jeff Morgan save Patrick Hilton's life, the delighted old prospector lets them join him on a mission to reclaim a gold nugget he left buried in an abandoned mine tunnel. But their quest goes awry when they reach the location only to find that it is now in the middle of the bustling mine at Copper Town.

The three men are already facing a race against time to find the gold before the tunnel re-opens, and their situation worsens when a gunslinger arrives to stake his claim for the nugget with hot lead. Now a stand-off develops – one in which the victors' prize will be the gold and the losers' fate will be a trip to Boot Hill. . . .

Stand-off at Copper Town

Scott Connor

A Black Horse Western

ROBERT HALE · LONDON

© Scott Connor 2010
First published in Great Britain 2011

ISBN 978-0-7090-9086-1

Robert Hale Limited
Clerkenwell House
Clerkenwell Green
London EC1R 0HT

www.halebooks.com

Typeset by
Derek Doyle & Associates, Shaw Heath
Printed and bound in Great Britain by
CPI Antony Rowe, Chippenham and Eastbourne

PROLOGUE

'Get out now,' Patrick Hilton shouted. 'The whole tunnel's coming down!'

As the last echo from Patrick's demand faded away, miners scurried past him with their heads down and their hands raised to ward off the patter of stones. Deeper into the tunnel the ground grumbled and timbers protested with a fatal insistence.

Patrick slapped every man's back while counting them out. But when the last miner ran by him he had only counted to five. Two men were still further back in the tunnel.

Patrick peered into the gloom, weighing up his chances if he were to go back in to find them. Ten feet away another timber strut snapped, the down-ward pressure making it explode across the tunnel and causing another collapse of dirt. On either side the walls were spitting pebbles, a sure sign that heading in any direction other than to ground level would be a fatal mistake.

But he went back anyhow.

He hurtled down the tunnel, rounded a corner, then skidded to a halt, his mouth falling open in shock. Ahead were the two remaining men, and they were fighting. Each man was trying to wrestle the other to the ground.

'Stop that and get out!' he shouted. 'Whatever this is about can wait.'

The men glanced at him, their eyes bright in the gloom. One man was Wallace Crowley, the other Foley Steele.

Patrick hurried on as Wallace dragged himself free of Foley's clutches and delivered a scything blow to his chin that crashed him backwards into the shaking tunnel wall. Then Wallace turned on his heel and took a pace away to head deeper into the tunnel.

Foley rebounded and lunged for him, gathering a fleeting hold of his arm before Wallace tore himself free then ran, quickly disappearing into the dust-shrouded gloom.

'Why has he gone down there?' Patrick demanded.

'Because the man's a damn fool,' Foley said, fingering his jaw. Then the ground shook, making him cringe, with his head down to his shoulders in fear.

They faced each other, silently debating their

next actions, not that they seriously considered heading to safety. These three men had prospected together for years and it'd been Wallace's idea to seek out and explore these old mine workings. No matter how stupid his actions were, they couldn't abandon him.

With a deep foreboding rumbling in his guts Patrick hurried down the tunnel with Foley trailing behind. He couldn't see his quarry, but the miners had been working a cramped opening to the side and Patrick presumed that was where Wallace had gone.

He knelt beside the opening's two-foot high entrance and peered into the darkness, seeing the dim smudge of candlelight bobbing around amidst the dust.

'Wallace,' he shouted, 'get out!'

'I just need a few more seconds,' Wallace said, grunting with effort.

'You haven't got a few more seconds,' Foley shouted.

'Just a—' Wallace didn't get to complete his comment as the tunnel then gave up its losing battle against the intolerable pressure.

Patrick and Foley did the only thing they could do and curled up with their arms held over their heads. For a seeming eternity they awaited their inevitable death while listening to the rocks and dirt cascade down.

After the crescendo of noise an eerie quietness descended.

Patrick drew in a cautious breath and despite the dust that made him cough, the lack of any weight pressing down on him sent his hopes soaring. He looked out from under an arm and the welcome sight of Foley's thumb-up signal greeted him.

Having enough light to see meant the whole tunnel hadn't collapsed and there would be a route out. It'd probably require them to crawl through a treacherously thin gap for a hundred yards, but at least they had a chance to escape that he hadn't thought they'd get a few seconds ago.

A hand slapped down on his shoulder and he turned to see the dim outline of a dirt-coated Wallace crawling into the space beside them, his rolled up jacket tucked under an arm.

'You ready to leave now?' Foley said, his tone terse.

'Sure am,' Wallace said, with a hint of laughter in his voice as he shuffled round to sit beside them.

'Then tell me one thing before we get out of here,' Patrick said. He took a deep breath to still the anger that was overcoming his shock. 'Why in tarnation did you fight with Foley, go back into a collapsing tunnel, and nearly get us all killed?'

Wallace didn't answer other than to offer a huge smile, then he pointed at his jacket. Slowly he took it out from under his arm and opened it up.

Patrick, then Foley looked at the revealed object

and couldn't help but join him in smiling.

Presently, a new, echoing sound reverberated in the tunnel: the three friends' gleeful laughter.

CHAPTER 1

'Hey!' Nathan Palmer shouted, coming to a halt on the boardwalk. 'Get your hands off him.'

The two men ignored him and continued to bundle the old-timer towards an alley. One man had an arm around their victim's waist while the other man pushed him onwards. The victim was struggling, but only feebly and his waving arms were brushing ineffectively against his assailants' bodies.

Nathan glanced at his friend Jeff Morgan, who rolled his shoulders.

'There's two of them,' Jeff said, 'and two of us. So I reckon we should have a quiet word with them.'

Nathan smiled when Jeff raised his fists showing what form that quiet word would take. Then, side-by-side, the two men paced down the boardwalk.

They had arrived in Snake Pass only ten minutes before. As it had been an hour after sundown they'd headed to a cheap eatery after which they'd planned to spend the evening roaming the saloons searching for news about any work that might be available. But this altercation had grabbed their attention first.

Although when Nathan got closer to the alley he saw that the old-timer had now given up on fighting back; his limp form was being dragged along with ease. When the assailants reached the entrance to the alley between the bank and a mercantile, they glanced back and saw that they were being followed.

They appraised Nathan's and Jeff's belligerent postures. One man stopped pushing the old-timer and swung round to confront them while the other man dragged their victim into the alley.

'Stay there,' the remaining man said. 'This don't concern you.'

Nathan and Jeff stomped to a halt before him.

'It will do unless you let him go,' Nathan said as Jeff cracked his knuckles for emphasis.

The man considered them with barely a flicker of concern, then moved aside his jacket to reveal a pearl-handled six-shooter.

'Two men who aren't packing guns don't tell me what to do.'

Nathan glanced at Jeff and raised his eyebrows. The man narrowed his eyes, clearly wondering what the signal had meant, but he found out that it had been only a distraction when Jeff darted in.

With a speed that was surprising for a large man he swung back both bunched fists then clattered them up and around in a ferocious blow to the chin that sent the man reeling away.

The man hit the corner of the alley where he hung on for a moment before sliding down the wall to land in a crumpled heap on the boardwalk. Then Jeff stood to one side of the alley while Nathan took the other.

'What's happening out there, Tucker?' the other man asked from within the dark alley.

Nathan caught Jeff's eye. They both nodded, confirming they'd await developments.

Rustling sounded within the alley. Then slow footfalls closed on the entrance.

'I said, what's—?'

The man didn't get to finish his question as he then emerged and met a swinging blow from Jeff's fist. At the last moment he saw it coming and moved aside, but he succeeded only in turning into a straight-armed jab from Nathan that crunched into his nose.

The man released the old-timer and staggered away, bleating in pain. While Jeff gave him the same treatment as Tucker had received, Nathan grabbed the former captive before he could fall over.

When the two would-be attackers were lying comatose and sprawled against each other on the boardwalk, Jeff stood over them in case they stirred while Nathan checked on the intended victim's condition.

'You fine, old-timer?' Nathan asked, lowering his head to consider his grizzled, bearded face.

'The name's Patrick Hilton,' he said groggily, 'and you just saved me the trouble of teaching them a lesson.'

Patrick smiled a weak and largely toothless grin, letting Nathan know he was exaggerating, but with him sounding in better condition than he'd feared, Nathan released him.

'Why were they trying to take you away?'

Patrick glanced at his attackers then while shaking his head he backed away for a pace to lean against the mercantile wall.

'It was my own fault, and if I had any money to repay your kindness, I'd treat you both to a meal and tell you about it.'

Jeff moved away from the unconscious attackers.

'Then why don't we buy you that meal,' he said, 'and you can still tell us about it.'

Patrick tipped back his hat to scratch his head in bemusement, perhaps finding it hard to trust them after his recent experience. But when both men nodded and gestured towards the eatery down the road, he patted them both on the back.

'In that case I'll tell you a tale that'll excite you so much it'll make your heads spin.'

Thirty minutes later Patrick had been true to his word and both men were staring at him agog. Their cleaned plates that had contained huge beefsteaks were pushed to one side, but their slices of apple pie were as yet untouched.

'And what was under Wallace Crowley's jacket when he opened it up?' Nathan asked.

'Wallace had dug up the largest nugget of gold I've ever seen.' Patrick pointed at the remnants of his pie before he speared another forkful. 'It was bigger than this piece of pie. Heck, it was bigger than the whole pie!'

Both men snorted at the possibility of this being true, but they still waited with bated breath until Patrick had swallowed the next mouthful.

'And what did you do with it?'

'And there's the point of my story.' Patrick forked the last piece of pie into his mouth then, while still chewing, he leaned forward. 'The tunnel started a-rumbling and a-shaking again. We had to get out quickly or die where we stood.'

'Did you get out?' Jeff asked, caught up in the story.

The other two men looked at him until he chuckled, realizing his mistake.

'*I* did,' Patrick said slowly. Then he leaned back in his chair with his mouth clamped shut, letting them complete the story.

Nathan nodded. 'So, what you're saying is that your two friends died and the gold nugget is still lying there in that collapsed mine tunnel?'

'You've got it. Digging through a hundred yards of

14

treacherous collapsed tunnel was a challenge for me and the rest of the prospectors who'd joined us on the expedition. But for that nugget it was worth it.' Patrick sighed, his eyes glazing as he appeared to think back to the events. 'And we'd almost reached it when it all went wrong. We were deep into bandit country and the bandits found us. We ran rather than get shot up, but I was the only one who survived to tell the story.'

'And after that?'

'After that,' Patrick said, his voice becoming sad for the first time, 'I've spent my life telling my story for food and whiskey. Except sometimes the people I tell it to want to hear the details I never divulge.'

'We saw that, but what I meant was, why didn't you go back for the nugget? This happened fifteen years ago and those bandits couldn't have been there for all that time.'

Patrick gave a quick shrug, although he wouldn't meet either man's eyes, suggesting he might be hiding something.

'I had other business to deal with, but now I'm back and this time I'm finally going on a mission to reclaim the nugget.' He rubbed his gums, locating a last morsel of pie before he favoured them with a huge grin. 'So I'm mighty obliged for your help.'

'And we're obliged for your story.'

Nathan caught Jeff's eye and they both smiled, silently acknowledging that neither of them believed the tall tale. Then Nathan reached over for his plate and began eating.

'And,' Jeff said, taking his plate, 'we both wish you well.'

Patrick looked from one man to the other then settled his gaze on their plates.

'I'll tell you some more for your portions of pie.'

Nathan laughed, spluttering a few crumbs.

'I'm enjoying the pie too much,' he said when he'd swallowed. 'But if you want another slice, just order one.'

Patrick lowered his head for a moment and then with a pensive expression he leaned back to ask for another slice to be sent over to their table. When it arrived, he poked at it, then considered them.

'You're really not interested in hearing the rest of my story, are you?'

'We enjoyed it,' Jeff said, finishing first. 'It was well worth the price of a meal. If there's any more to it, tell us, but make it quick as we have to start touring the saloons.'

'We've got work to find,' Nathan said.

'And quickly before our money runs out,' Jeff added.

Patrick looked at his pie and gulped.

'You probably saved my life and then you used your own meagre funds to buy me a meal. You two are good men.'

'Let's hope we can find someone who's hiring who

16

thinks that too.'

Patrick stabbed his fork down into his pie with a determined gesture and beamed at them.

'He does,' he said.

Nathan gulped down the last of his pie, but before he could ask who, Jeff caught on to what he meant.

'You?' he asked.

Patrick nodded. 'I reckon after tonight's experience I'd be wise to hire two strong, trustworthy men.'

'But you said you don't have any money.'

'I don't now, but I will have soon.' Patrick carved off a large forkful of pie. 'And then I'll cut you a slice that'll repay the cost of this meal a thousand times over.'

'Are you sure about this, Nathan?' Jeff asked when the old-timer had gone to sleep.

With them having spent all their money on supplies, they'd had no choice about where they would sleep that night and so had headed out of town and made camp. Since accepting Patrick's offer they'd not yet had a chance to talk privately, but with the old-timer snoring like a howling coyote Nathan considered.

'Nope,' he said. 'In all honesty, while we were eating, I thought Patrick's tale was a tall one to keep us entertained, and I still think that.'

Jeff gestured at their supply-laden horses and Patrick's collection of equipment.

'Then why are we out here?'

'Because I'd hate to hear later that we got it wrong and Patrick's become a rich man.'

Jeff laughed and locked his hands behind his head.

'I guess it'll be an adventure. If it leads nowhere, all we've lost is a few weeks, and we'll be exactly where we were before we went searching for a huge nugget of gold.'

'And we may even get ourselves a story we can tell others for whiskey and a meal.'

As Jeff nodded then leaned back against his saddle, Nathan settled down against his own saddle. On his back he looked up at the stars, imagining that every one of them was a speck of gold.

CHAPTER 2

'Are we close?' Nathan asked when they'd settled down for the night after another long day's riding.

Patrick waved the map that he'd consulted on every night of their ten-day journey so far.

'I reckon,' he said, 'we should get there tomorrow.'

Jeff moved round the camp-fire to peer at the map.

'Where are we?' he asked, craning his neck.

As usual Patrick flinched away to keep the map out of sight. Despite their agreement, he viewed the specifics of his hard-earned information as being secret. Questions about what problems they might encounter on the way and what they would find when they got there were always met with silence or an unsubtle change of subject.

'You can trust us,' Nathan said, smiling.

Patrick considered the smile then cast a shamefaced look at each man in turn.

'I'm sorry, but everybody I've met has tried to find out what I know, usually using the same way as those two men back in Snake Pass. But I should accept that you two are different.'

Nathan nodded. 'We're not going to kill you or abandon you out here. We'll do nothing but take our share.'

Patrick looked at them guardedly. 'And you don't mind getting the smaller share?'

Nathan could see that this issue was important to him and that this was why he had yet to trust them completely. So he took a while to reply and then lowered his voice to an honest tone.

'We accepted your deal. You take half of whatever we find and we share the other half.' He spread his hands. 'It's a more than fair deal when you have all the information and a fair claim to it all, and we have only our hands to help you dig it out.'

'It is, but gold does strange things to a man. You may say that now, but once you can touch it, feel it, smell it, taste it. . . .' Patrick licked his lips with a look that said in his prospecting days he hadn't been immune to duplicitous thoughts himself.

'Not us. So you can stop looking for deception here and concentrate on looking for trouble coming from elsewhere.'

Patrick considered. Then, with a slap of his thighs, he spread the map out on the ground and beckoned them to sit around him.

'We're moving beside this ridge,' he said, jabbing a finger against the centre of the map then moving it upwards. 'And we're heading here.'

As Nathan knew nothing about the area, he orientated himself by locating Snake Pass in the bottom corner of the map. Jeff gestured at the area ahead.

'Isn't Copper Town out here somewhere?' he asked.

Patrick shrugged. 'Not heard of it.'

'I don't know much about it either, but I'd heard they'd built a railroad up to it from Ash Creek.' He pointed at the small town in the bottom left-hand corner.

Patrick hurriedly rolled up the map and slipped it away.

'You're wrong. This is wild country. We're the only people within a hundred miles of this spot.'

'You're right that we haven't seen anybody since leaving Snake Pass,' Nathan said. 'But that's an old map. Things might have changed.'

Patrick pouted then stomped away to his blanket. He dragged it up to his neck and rolled over to face away from them showing they wouldn't get any more answers out of him that night.

Nathan had no reason not to believe him, but the next day he started to wonder. He'd become used to the sounds around them: the clop of hoofs on the gritty ground, the creaking and jangling of Patrick's equipment, the occasional distant animal or bird noise.

As the day wore on he briefly heard other noises: a hum and distant susurration that was almost too low to hear, but which suggested people were about. The three men frequently glanced at each other then at the landscape searching for the source of the noise, but it remained distant and undefined.

In mid afternoon they crossed a river, providing a possible reason for the noise. Buffaloberry and aspen bordered the river, the pleasant locale encouraging them to dally for a while, but when they moved on the low sounds grew in volume. Gradually they moved to higher ground on the ridge and from what he could remember about the map, Nathan identified a massive rocky outcrop as their destination.

They negotiated a snaking path up the ridge and when they emerged before the main bulk of rock they found signs of industrial activity. The side of the outcrop had been blasted and chipped away to create a sheer stretch of rock with a flat area at the bottom. To their left this area continued down a slight incline around the side of the outcrop until it disappeared from view. In the other direction the flattened area ended abruptly two hundred and fifty yards away.

'This wasn't here the last time,' Patrick said, eyeing the flat ground with contempt. 'Someone must have done some work here after I left.'

'A long time after you left,' Nathan said, leaning from the saddle to peer at the ground. 'The rocks are sharp and unweathered. This is recent work.'

As if to prove his point the low background noise peaked, giving him the impression of raised voices; they sounded as if they were coming from ahead.

The group cast bemused glances at each other then moved over the flattened area. At the base of the outcrop they dismounted and searched for the best place to climb.

They had to head to the end of the flat area to find a spot where the route upwards was climbable. Even then they had to clamber up 200 feet of rock on hands and feet to traverse the lowest point of the ridge. The closer they got to the summit, the louder the background noise became.

There were voices along with the clang of metal on metal punctuated by the rumble of earth moving. With increasing trepidation they closed in on the summit and when the view beyond came into sight they stared down in wonderment.

A small town was below; hundreds of men were demolishing the outcrop; numerous tunnels had been bored into the ground and around them a steady stream of men and burros were moving back and forth.

Rocks were being carried out of the tunnels while a production process ground them down before carrying them on to buildings for smelting. To their side they could see that the flattened area had been created to house railroad tracks that made their way up towards them before stopping beside the town.

'What in tarnation is this?' Patrick murmured unhappily.

'I reckon,' Jeff said, 'this is Copper Town.'

'What are you people doing here?'

The question had come from a man who was somewhat cleaner than most of the workers, so Nathan presumed he was in authority.

Nathan and Jeff moved back to let Patrick speak, but before he did he cast another forlorn look over the area, taking in the numerous mine workings that must surely have wiped out the landscape with which he was familiar.

For a moment his gaze alighted on a high point on the outcrop. A small smile appeared.

'We're looking for work,' he said.

'We recruit in Ash Creek. Nobody comes here looking for work. In fact I've never seen nobody coming out here looking for anything.' He glanced at Patrick's horse and chuckled. 'Except for a few idiots who'd heard about the old mine workings and believed those damn-fool stories about the gold here.'

The overseer licked his lips in anticipation of getting more amusement out of Patrick's response, but he didn't rise to the bait.

24

'Do you have work, or not?'

The overseer sighed. Then, with his hands on his hips, he looked them over.

'I am short of a few men right now. With water being more precious here than the gold people used to come looking for, I need an extra water detail.'

He pointed, signifying a wagon laden down with barrels then a route over the rail tracks that led back the way they had come to the nearby river.

They thanked him then moved over to the wagon. Only when they were out of earshot did Nathan ask the question that he was sure was also on Jeff's mind.

'We didn't come here looking for work,' he said. 'So why are we now working on a water detail?'

Patrick winked then jerked his head towards a high point on the outcrop.

'Don't let anyone see you looking that way, but I've seen the place where I was the last time.' Patrick chuckled. 'And they haven't ruined that area yet. The tunnel with the gold nugget in it is still here.'

CHAPTER 3

There was only enough time before sundown for one journey down to the river. This was fine with Nathan as they'd had a long and irritating day.

When they returned to the mine the overseer who had employed them, Sherman Clarke, directed them to one of the large communal tents where they could sleep. He'd found someone to take care of their horses, but his sly smile as they were led away didn't give Nathan any confidence that he would see them again.

Patrick ignored his concern. He had been getting more animated as the afternoon wore on and he got closer to completing his quest.

'What's the plan?' Jeff asked when they'd collected their meal from the chuck wagon.

'We wait until dark,' Patrick said while glancing around to check nobody was paying them undue attention. 'Then we go for a walk and see what's here.'

They said nothing more on the matter and instead gravitated towards the workers and exchanged pleasantries. The tiredness and strain was clear in the miners' eyes, but everyone was prepared to pass on the rules of Copper Town.

You worked hard, did what you were told, and that earned you a few hours of freedom to enjoy yourself in Copper Town. That enjoyment involved gambling, rough liquor, and even rougher women.

Although Marshal Lawton confiscated weapons that were brought within the town limits, fights and even killings were common. But they welcomed the news. It meant everyone would be too preoccupied to notice what they got up to.

They still mingled in with the main bulk of men heading to town, but they stopped on the outskirts of the area of clapboard buildings and small tents. They waited until nobody was left to follow them then veered away.

At a slow pace while engaged in animated conversation that gave the impression they had nothing to hide, they headed to the railroad tracks. They stopped and sat on a boulder then looked beyond the tracks towards the distant river, making it look as if they were whiling away their time aimlessly.

After a half-hour nobody had come close. So, by the light of the low moon and the fires lit around the outskirts of town, they headed past the end of the tracks to the place where they'd first seen the town.

They climbed. Patrick took the lead, clambering over rocks towards his goal with an assurance that gave Nathan confidence that he remembered the area.

They didn't speak as the area gradually opened up below and let them see the full extent of the workings; clearly the mine had been spreading for some time. For hundred of yards beyond the town the ground was pitted and devastated, but closer to the area hadn't been worked on so much.

'They're working uphill,' Patrick said, gesturing at the tracks, 'and gradually coming this way.'

'Then we got here just in time,' Nathan said. 'In another few weeks, perhaps even days, they'll reach your tunnel.'

Patrick nodded then bade them to be silent and concentrate on their own safety as they traversed the last section. After ten minutes of climbing, they came out on the highest summit of the ridge.

From here they could see that the ridge followed a sweeping curve, which ultimately swung round to join the outcrop on both sides. Effectively this created a cauldron-shaped hollow before the outcrop.

Behind them was the town and ahead was the outcrop. To the right the ridge was thin and crumbling. To the left the ridge lowered into a gully that was filled with rocks, perhaps from a recent landslide.

On all sides the terrain was so steep the moonlight couldn't penetrate into the darkness below. Patrick pointed out their destination on the outcrop as being a high point with several indentations, these presumably being old tunnels that had collapsed.

With the ridge close to the outcrop appearing treacherous, they set off into the blackness of the cauldron, but while the upper half of his body was still in the light, Nathan stood on a rock that slipped away. He had an uncomfortable moment where he panicked and waved his arms feeling as if he would go tumbling.

His foot landed on solid ground further down the slope and he fetched up with a lurch. Adding to his discomfort the rock then landed at the bottom with a dull thud, having made no sound on its way down.

Jeff grabbed his arm righting him, but his motion dragged them both forward and the two men teetered until they found their equilibrium.

They stood awkwardly until Nathan sat to rest and flex his ankle. It was fine, but when he looked up Patrick was shaking his head.

'You two aren't used to clambering over rocks,' he said. 'Stay here and watch for anyone approaching. I'll head to the outcrop alone.'

Without complaint, Nathan and Jeff stood back to let him leave. Then, as he disappeared into the darkness, they settled down to await news.

Jeff looked towards the town while Nathan faced

the outcrop. He considered the indentations, wondering which one interested Patrick. They all looked the same to him and Patrick had given them no clues.

Thirty minutes passed with the only sounds being the swell of noise coming from Copper Town as the miners enjoyed themselves after a long day, and the clang of metal in the smelting sheds that never stopped working. Both men were becoming restless when Patrick finally appeared from out of the darkness and worked his way up the slope.

He clambered past the first row of collapsed tunnels and was fifty feet below the end one in the second row when Jeff nudged him.

'Trouble,' he whispered.

Nathan turned. Below, a line of five riders was making its way from the town along the railroad tracks. As Nathan and Jeff were hiding in the shadows they wouldn't be able to see them up on the ridge, but they were steering a course directly towards them.

Nathan glanced at the riders then at Patrick who was still climbing slowly.

'If they are coming up here,' he said, 'it'll take them a while to get up the ridge. Patrick should be finished by then.'

'Hopefully, but I reckon we should still warn him.'

Jeff hefted a small stone then moved over to the other side of the ridge and launched it towards

Patrick. The stone disappeared quietly into the blackness, so Nathan joined him in throwing.

The distance proved to be too great for them to reach Patrick and all the stones fell into the inky blackness and made no discernible sound, but Patrick must have heard a noise, as he flinched. He looked down then up towards them.

While keeping below the top of the ridge, they waved frantically then pointed towards town. Patrick acknowledged them with a wave and so Jeff raised a hand then pointed at his fingers signifying that five riders were coming.

Patrick provided a non-committed shrug, suggesting he didn't know what he meant. Then he waved a dismissive hand at them and moved up the slope, but he clambered with a greater sense of urgency.

Nathan and Jeff did the only thing they could do and kept track of his progress and of the men below. When the riders reached a point below them they stopped and talked amongst themselves. Their urgent tones travelled up to them on the night air, but no words were intelligible.

Nathan recognized Sherman Clarke, the overseer, amongst the group. The others nodded attentively while he gestured at the ridge. Once he'd given his orders, the other four men climbed, using broadly the same route as Nathan and the others had taken earlier.

'This is looking bad,' Jeff said when it became

obvious they wouldn't veer away and were climbing towards their position.

Nathan nodded. Despite their attempts to be stealthy, it appeared that they had been seen and these men had come to investigate. He looked over his shoulder, but to his irritation Patrick had disappeared from view, presumably into the tunnel he'd been climbing towards.

'The moment Patrick comes out,' he said, 'he has to find somewhere to hide. But we can't hang around to make sure he does. We need to move now.'

Jeff grunted that he agreed and so without further debate they picked their way along the summit. They resisted the urge to check on the climbing men's progress as they traversed a rocky path that would take them about fifty yards away from Sherman.

Nathan was wondering whether Patrick would be better served staying hidden when he emerged from the end tunnel. He walked stiffly, looking towards the ridge opposite, but not at the position where they'd been before.

Nathan and Jeff stopped and grabbed a handful of stones, but before they could throw them and gather his attention, Nathan saw the reason why he wasn't looking for them.

Two other men were edging out of the tunnel behind him, and both had guns trained on his back.

'We'll never get through all these people,' Jeff said.

'But why are they here?' Nathan said. 'Surely nobody will be interested in what Patrick was doing last night.'

'Perhaps something else happened later. In a town like this, I'm sure the jailhouse is always full of rowdy drunks and fighters.'

Nathan nodded. Then they started working their way through the press of people.

The night before, after seeing that they couldn't help Patrick, they'd made the sensible decision to hide in the shadows until he had been led away. Then, while Sherman's group were moving round the ridge to collect him, they'd taken a roundabout route down to the railroad tracks and then to their tent where they'd listened out for news.

They'd heard nothing until first light when the first shift had stirred, but instead of starting work everyone had gravitated towards town. Jeff and Nathan had joined them and found they were congregating outside the building that served as the marshal's office and jailhouse.

They mingled, hoping to hear what the trouble was, and got their answer when they saw Sherman making his way through the throng. They avoided looking at him, but he headed straight for them. When he stopped, he looked them up and down, then pointed at the law office.

'You're coming with me,' he said.

With Sherman walking behind them, they headed

on. At first they had to push people aside to make headway, but soon everyone got the idea that Sherman wanted to get through and a gap appeared ahead.

Nathan avoided catching anyone's eye, but most people were more interested in getting out of Sherman's way than in noticing who had attracted his ire. When they reached the office, they went straight in. Marshal Lawton had a desk beside the door with a row of large cells filling most of the office.

Nathan looked along the cells, but he couldn't see Patrick amongst the incarcerated men. Most of the men were sleeping on the floor or were sitting with their heads in their hands looking sour and battered and so suggesting a reason why they were there.

Sherman signified they should stand to the side while he faced Lawton.

'Plot foiled, then?' Lawton asked.

'There's been no more trouble since last night,' Sherman said. He glanced at the cells. 'He tell you anything useful?'

'Nope.' Lawton gestured towards the endmost cell. 'His lips are clamped tight.'

The end cell was the only one not seething with prisoners and was set a short distance from the nearest cell. The mingling mass of men parted for long enough to let Nathan see that Patrick was sitting there alone.

'Keep working on him. I need to know the names of his accomplices.' Sherman cast Nathan and Jeff a significant glance and raised his eyebrows inviting them to talk, but both men remained silent. 'He rode into Copper Town yesterday with these two.'

Lawton swung round on his chair to consider them with a steady appraising gaze.

'And yet only now do you bring them to me.'

'I was keeping them under watch.' Sherman joined him in considering them. 'And besides, they claim they came here looking for gold, not the payroll.'

'We don't know nothing about no payroll,' Nathan said, deciding he couldn't keep his silence. His voice emerged with a high-pitched tone, but he consoled himself with the thought that it sounded innocent. 'We did come here prospecting, but Patrick had got it wrong, so we decided to work instead. I guess Patrick was still unconvinced and he went scouting around for gold.'

Sherman folded his arms. 'He wasn't scouting around when we found him. He was trying to steal the payroll I've secured out on the outcrop.'

'We don't know nothing about that.' Nathan considered Sherman's sceptical expression, then brightened. 'You saw the equipment we brought.'

'I did. Some might think it was excellent cover for what you were really doing, and some might think it was an excellent collection of tools to steal the payroll.'

Nathan looked at Jeff for help in explaining themselves, but he returned a sorry shake of the head that
said Sherman wouldn't believe anything they said.

Nathan set his hands on his hips. 'What can we say
to convince you that Patrick's innocent?'

'That's a good question, and it's one you can
discuss with the marshal from the other side of the
bars.'

Nathan opened his mouth to reply, but before he
could speak Marshal Lawton coughed.

'Why would I arrest these men?' he asked. 'You
have no proof.'

Sherman narrowed his eyes and slapped both
hands down on the desk to peer at the lawman, who
returned his gaze with calm ease. His mouth opened
and closed as he struggled for words.

'What more do you want?' he snapped. 'A stolen
payroll?'

'That would be your concern, but I'd still want
more proof than you've shown me to arrest them for
taking it.'

Sherman snorted under his breath, but then, with
a slap of a fist against his thigh, he swirled round to
face Nathan.

'It's lucky for you that I'm a fair man,' he muttered, 'so get back to work. I've put two new men on
your water detail. Show them what to do and stay
away from the outcrop. I'm watching you and if you
go within a hundred yards of the payroll, I won't wait

for Lawton to arrest you. I'll deal with you myself.'

With that promise he barged between them and headed outside where he immediately stopped to glare at the gathering. With a few broad gestures, he shooed everyone away and urged them to start work.

'Obliged,' Jeff said with a sigh of relief.

Lawton leaned back in his chair. 'Don't be. The only reason I'm not arresting you is to annoy Sherman.'

'I don't understand,' Nathan said.

Lawton got to his feet then went to the window to look out at the dispersing crowd.

'It means I want to believe you.' Lawton turned and flashed a smile. 'Find out what's going on here – and I will.'

As Nathan narrowed his eyes, Jeff joined Lawton at the window.

'If you're making us an offer, you'd better spell it out.'

Lawton nodded, but he didn't reply immediately as he collected his thoughts.

'Rumours are spreading about miners going missing,' he said, speaking slowly. 'But nobody will talk and I don't even have names.'

'That sounds mighty troubling,' Nathan said, 'but we only arrived yesterday. It's got nothing to do with us.'

'It has now. If you want Patrick released, find out what's going on in Copper Town. Find out who's gone missing, then find out why and who did it.'

Nathan glanced at the end cell. 'And if we don't find out, we'll end up in a cell with Patrick?'

'Nope. If you don't find out, you'll beg me to put you in a cell.' As Nathan and Jeff furrowed their brows in confusion, Lawton waved at the window, signifying the departing crowd. 'They gathered because they'd heard someone had tried to steal the payroll. In a town like this, such rumours can end in a lynching. So one word from me and you won't live to see another sundown.'

'We understand,' Nathan said. Then, with Lawton offering no more explanations, they turned to the door. 'We'll talk later.'

'You will,' Lawton said. 'I want names.'

Outside they were pleased to see that nearly everyone had departed, so they walked slowly to the water wagon. They said nothing on the way.

As promised two new men were waiting for them. They were leaning on the wagon, slouching and not looking enthused about the work they'd been allocated. Nathan reckoned he'd seen them before. He wasn't sure where, but when they detected their approach both men looked up and smiled in a sly way that suggested they also recognized them.

They also murmured to each other before peeling away to face them. Nathan waved at them to climb up on the wagon, but neither man moved.

'We're late leaving already,' Nathan said. 'Hurry up.'

38

The nearest man smirked and licked his lips.

'You claiming you don't remember us?' he snarled.

Nathan replayed the last words through his mind and with a sudden jolt he realized where he'd heard the voice before.

'You're the gunslingers from Snake Pass,' he murmured.

'We sure are.'

Both men paced up to confront him as Jeff winced with recognition. One man ruefully rubbed his jaw while the other rubbed his stomach, remembering the places where they'd been hit.

'And this time,' the second man said, 'you won't surprise us in the dark.'

'What do you want with us?' Nathan asked, still bemused that they had travelled so far to repay being bettered.

'We want the gold the old-timer claimed was here. If we don't get it, you'll both get what you avoided back in Snake Pass.'

CHAPTER 4

The journey to the river was a slow one.

The four men hadn't hurried in their duties and after Tucker Jeffords and Clay Meeker, as they now knew them, had delivered their threats, none of them had spoken again. But when Nathan caught his first sight of the river, their two unwelcome co-workers shuffled closer to the seat in the back of the wagon.

'Is this the only trip we have to make today?' Tucker asked.

Nathan didn't reply immediately, wondering if this was a prelude to more threats, but he figured that despite their mutual animosity they still had a job to do.

'When we return, we get a break for them to remove the barrels. Then we head back to the river again and keep on going back and forth until sundown.'

'Then we'll have to wait,' Clay said, 'until dark before you get us the gold.'

Nathan concentrated on steering a straight course beside the railroad tracks leaving Jeff to lean back and reply.

'It's not that simple.' Jeff gestured around, taking in the out-of-view town, railroad, and mine. 'Patrick got it wrong. This place is no longer the one he explored fifteen years ago. We've all wasted our time over a tall tale.'

Clay sneered. 'We're not listening to no excuses. We will leave with the gold.'

Jeff and Nathan looked at each other and shrugged then concentrated on steering the wagon, judging that nothing they could say would placate these men.

When they arrived at the water, Clay and Tucker took one look at the work to be done then drifted away, leaving Jeff and Nathan to unload the barrels, but this was fine with them. It let them talk privately for the first time since they'd joined up with the others.

'What we going to do?' Jeff asked after dragging the first barrel to the top of the planks.

'Is that in finding out why people are going missing,' Nathan said, gesturing for Jeff to release the barrel so that it'd roll down to the ground, 'or in dealing with Tucker and Clay?'

Jeff snorted a laugh then kicked the barrel down.

41

'One of those problems would be bad enough, but I guess we have to resolve them both.'

Nathan slowed the barrel to a halt then considered the two surly men, who were standing back and eyeing them from under lowered hats on the edge of the water.

'In that case we have to sort out our hardest problem first. And as I reckon Marshal Lawton can't expect us to solve his mystery quickly, that means getting rid of these two.'

'Agreed.'

Jeff kicked down a second barrel. This time Nathan didn't stop it and let it roll on until it came to a halt beside Tucker and Clay.

Tucker gave the barrel an irritated kick then looked up at them.

'What have you decided after your whispering?' he asked.

'That we should talk about our problem,' Nathan said. He flexed his fists while Jeff jumped down from the wagon and rolled his shoulders.

Tucker and Clay both backed away for a cautious pace towards the river. Tucker glanced down at his empty holster.

'You two sound mighty brave when we're unarmed, but remember that we will get our weapons back when we leave.'

Nathan smiled, being relieved for the first time that Lawton strictly enforced his policy of not letting the miners pack guns. He advanced on Tucker while Jeff paced up to Clay.

'You had guns last time but it didn't help you, so it sure won't help you this time.'

Tucker took another backwards pace, but on the slippery edge of the water his foot slipped. Nathan made him pay for his piece of bad luck and hurried in.

He threw his weight behind a two-handed clubbing blow to his cheek that cracked his head to the side. Tucker stumbled backwards for a pace.

Nathan followed through with a blow from the other direction that sent Tucker into the water. A contemptuous push made him slip. He fell, landing with a huge splash, then floundered in the shallows with his arms and legs splayed in an undignified fashion.

He pushed, trying to regain his footing, but he slipped again and landed on his rump. Slowly he sat up in the water and glared at Nathan standing on the riverside.

'You just made a big mistake,' he muttered, as he rolled on to his knees.

'I don't reckon so. Twice we've tussled and twice you've been flattened. Maybe you'll get yourself some sense and not try for a third time.'

While keeping an eye on Tucker, Nathan edged backwards giving him a chance to back down. Tucker didn't make a move to reach him and Nathan soon found out why.

'Stop there,' Clay said, 'or this one dies.'

Nathan winced. He hadn't paid attention to how Jeff was faring with Clay, assuming his friend would best him.

He looked over his shoulder. Clay had pressed a knife to Jeff's neck, his hunched posture and glaring eyes suggesting he would have no compunction about digging the knife in. Jeff was standing rigidly with his hands slightly raised.

'He had a hidden knife,' Jeff said.

'And he'll lower it,' Nathan muttered. 'We don't respond to threats.'

Unseen by Clay, Jeff widened his eyes and gulped, clearly asking him if he was sure about his gamble. Nathan avoiding catching his eye, and to his relief Tucker clambered out of the water and waved at Clay to lower the knife.

'Do what he says,' he said.

Clay's biceps flexed as he appeared to consider defiance, but then, after a muttered comment to himself, he lowered the knife. As Jeff breathed a sigh of relief, Nathan gestured for Clay and Tucker to join him at the wagon, but before anyone could move a slow hand clap sounded.

The four men swirled round to find that Sherman Clarke was standing on the back of the wagon looking down at them having arrived unheard while they'd been fighting. He continued clapping even when he had everyone's attention. Then, with a smile on his lips, he jumped down to join them.

'Now that,' he said, holding out a hand for the knife, 'sure was interesting. I thought you'd be planning something down here, but I didn't expect you'd be cutting each other up. Anyone want to tell me why?'

Tucker joined Nathan, and after Clay had handed over the knife, in an apparent show of solidarity that Nathan wouldn't have expected a few moments ago, he stood beside Jeff.

'We were discussing the best way to load up the wagon,' Tucker said, wringing water out of his jacket.

'It was a lively discussion,' Jeff added.

Despite their previous argument, Nathan smiled and even Clay managed a nonchalant stance, leaving Sherman to cast suspicious glares at them.

'Then you've wasted your breath. I let you leave the mine to find out what you were up to, but the answer has turned out to be a disappointing one. So as this is the softest job here and there's plenty of good men in line to do it, I reckon it's time I gave you some' – Sherman licked his lips and smirked – 'some special duties instead.'

The main mine workings were below the outcrop, but the steady progress onward would soon be making inroads into the huge slab of rock. The bulk of the work was veering towards the boulder-strewn gully they had seen the previous night from high up on the ridge. Without the boulders it would provide a convenient passage to the cauldron into which Patrick had climbed down.

Sherman told them that a rockslide a month before had filled the gully with a jumble of boulders and so the area had been deemed too dangerous to investigate until it had been cleared. Nobody had been prepared to volunteer to do that clearing, until now.

'What do you want us to do?' Clay asked.

Sherman merely snorted. Then, with brief gestures, he ordered Tucker and Clay to bring a large box to him.

Despite some surly muttered comments, the two men did as ordered. On the way back to the mine nobody had discussed their situation, but Nathan had no doubt that when Sherman left them alone they would resume their unfinished business.

When Sherman opened the box they saw what was expected of them. Nathan wasn't surprised that Tucker led the complaints.

'I've never used dynamite before,' he grumbled. 'This looks dangerous.'

'Don't worry,' Sherman said. 'Everybody back in the mine will be safe.'

'But you must have someone who's better qualified to do this.'

'I have. But they've all worked here longer than you have.'

46

As Tucker snorted, acknowledging the humour, Nathan stepped forward, judging that no amount of complaining would get them out of this task.

'Where do we start?' he asked.

Sherman pointed at the nearest boulders.

'There,' he said. 'Then keep going until the boulders are small enough to be dragged away and we can access the area beyond.'

Nathan reached into the box and took a stick, then hefted it on the palm of his hand.

'Do we get any more instructions, or are you leaving us to blow ourselves up?'

Sherman didn't reply immediately, but then to everyone's relief he deemed that he'd dragged enough entertainment out of their discomfort and took pity on them.

For the next half-hour he explained how they should plant the sticks and light the fuses and the kind of areas they should seek to plant them in for maximum effect.

After a last warning not to fritter away their time as there were tasks he could give them that were even more dangerous than this one, Sherman left them. When he'd disappeared from view, Tucker cast a significant glance at the box of dynamite then turned to face Nathan and Jeff.

'We have a job to do,' he said, 'but we can still finish what we started.'

Jeff raised his fists, eager for a re-match after being

bested the last time, but Nathan kept his own fists down.

'We'll admit that there could be gold here,' he said, deciding that some honesty would be the best way of putting an end to what could develop into an endless series of confrontations. 'Except we don't know for sure as the only person who does know is Patrick, the old-timer you attacked.'

Tucker nodded. 'Where is he?'

'Marshal Lawton arrested him for trying to steal the mine payroll.'

Tucker and Clay both narrowed their eyes with scepticism.

'Patrick told a good story. You don't.'

'We're not telling a story. Ask any of the miners. They all know about his arrest.'

Tucker shrugged. 'Did he do it?'

'Of course he didn't. He was searching for the gold.'

'Where?'

'We don't know. He wouldn't let us go with him. So that means you now know as much as we do about the gold. If you want to find out where he looked, you need to talk to him.' Nathan smiled. 'And the only way you can do that is to prove his innocence and get him released.'

Tucker opened his mouth, presumably to continue questioning him, but then closed it and with a resigned air he slouched towards the gully.

'We'll think about what you said,' he said. 'For now, we blow up rocks.'

'I don't like this,' Clay said, joining him with his expression set in a scowl. 'There's an awful smell around here.'

'There's an awful smell everywhere,' Nathan said. 'You'll get used to it.'

Clay continued to shuffle uncomfortably, and when Jeff joined him, he wrinkled his nose too.

'He's right,' he said. He beckoned Nathan to follow him to the gully. He stopped before the rocks and raised his head as he sniffed. 'Something's died here.'

Nathan sniffed then nodded as the unmistakable reek of an animal long dead wafted by him. They split up to search the area, but after only a minute of peering around the boulders, Jeff cried out.

They gathered around as he emerged from between two large boulders with his upper lip curled in disgust. Nathan moved to see what he'd found, but Jeff shook his head, saying the sight wouldn't do him much good, then hurried off to find help.

Ten minutes later he returned with Sherman Clarke in tow along with Miles Yates, Sherman's immediate subordinate.

Miles was the first to venture an identification of the body that Jeff reckoned had been crammed down between the two boulders for a while.

'It's Baxter Meredith,' he said.

'Baxter!' Sherman said. 'It can't be. I paid Baxter his wages four days ago, and that man has been dead for at least a week.'

CHAPTER 5

'What's going on here?' Tucker asked.

'I don't know,' Nathan said. 'But that's what we're supposed to find out.'

'And finding this body,' Jeff added, 'is sure to help Marshal Lawton.'

Sherman was still exploring the area where they'd found the body, giving them a breather before they had to start work, but the break had only rekindled their new associates' argumentative nature.

'I don't care who that dead man was,' Clay grumbled. 'I just want the gold and unless I get it someone is going to pay.'

Clay glared at Jeff then Nathan, but both men shook their heads then turned to the more reasonable Tucker.

'Everything we've told you is the truth,' Nathan said, 'and so what you do now is up to you.'

As everything they'd said had been true, except

51

for the details they'd left out, Nathan put on the most honest smile he could manage. Tucker gnawed at his lip as he considered them, then gave a firm shake of the head.

'We're staying,' he said, 'but we're not helping you get the old-timer out of jail. We'll get answers our way.'

With that statement of intent, he swung round to watch Miles and Sherman until they'd completed their discussion.

Presently two more men arrived to take the body away, but not before Sherman had issued the foursome with orders to make up for the lost time.

'What we going to do, then?' Jeff asked as they followed Tucker and Clay back to the gully.

'I guess we're on our own,' Nathan said.

Jeff breathed a sigh of relief. 'At least something has gone right today.'

'Do you know Baxter Meredith?' Nathan asked.

The man turned from the bar to cast him a brief and surly consideration.

'Nope.'

The man swung away to lean over his whiskey with a determined gesture that said the discussion was over. Nathan didn't mind. So far tonight everyone had behaved like this.

After he'd asked two more men without success, Jeff returned from his end of the bar shaking his head.

'Nobody knows anything about Baxter,' he said.

'Nobody knows anything about anything!' Nathan said.

Jeff sighed. 'I guess that's why Lawton was desperate enough to hire us.'

Before they left Nathan cast his measured gaze around the saloon. There were four such establishments in town and they'd worked their way around three without luck. Neither had they found anyone who had been prepared to talk back at the mine nor while they'd queued at the chuck wagon.

Despite the lack of interest in talking about the dead man, Nathan judged that the miners were in better spirits than Lawton had implied. People were chatting in numerous small groups with the silence and suspicion starting only when they asked questions.

'Maybe we're going about this the wrong way,' Nathan said.

'That's clear,' Jeff said with a laugh, 'but I can't think of any other way.'

Nathan said nothing more until they reached the final saloon on the road. This proved to be a quieter place, possibly because it was furthest away from the mine.

The establishment was beside the station and was constructed solidly, suggesting it might have been one of the first buildings to be erected. It even had chairs and tables around which games of poker were in progress.

53

As usual they headed to the bar.

'We've found something valuable,' Nathan said to the first man he approached, 'but we can't find its owner.'

'I should be able to help,' the man said, swinging away from the bar with a smile and showing more enthusiasm than anyone else had all night.

'It belongs to Baxter Meredith.'

The man rubbed his chin and looked aloft, giving the impression of pondering.

'I know Baxter.' He held out a hand. 'Let me have it and I'll pass it on to him.'

Nathan folded his arms. 'How well do you know him?'

'Well enough not to steal from him.'

'When did you last see him?'

'Must have been this morning, but I'll see him again soon.' He thrust out his hand with the fingers splayed and his jaw set firm as if more questions would offend him.

'Then you'll have a shock. Baxter's dead, been dead for a while in fact. But we found something on him and we thought we should give it to a friend of his.' Nathan leaned forward. 'So, are you a friend or not?'

The man gnawed his bottom lip while he appeared to weigh up the risks and benefits, but then with a dismissive wave of the hand he turned back to the bar.

Despite the failure, Nathan judged that this method had received a more promising response than before. So, meaning to try again, he moved to head down the bar, but then he found that two men had come over to stand beside him.

'You're asking about Baxter Meredith,' the nearest man said.

'We are,' Nathan said, flinching back in surprise at getting this response after so many setbacks. He judged that the two men were older than most of the miners, and so perhaps these grizzled veterans weren't as suspicious as the others were.

'How did he die?' the second man said, stepping up to join the other and encouraging Jeff to step closer to Nathan in case of trouble.

'Don't know,' Jeff said. 'But apparently he's been dead for over a week.'

The two men glanced at each other, seeming with a raised eyebrow and a returned shrug to exchange information silently as only people who knew each other well could.

'Then that explains why we haven't seen him for a while.'

'Do you know,' the second man asked, 'anything about Peter Parsons? He was with Baxter the last time we saw him.'

'No, but we gathered that Baxter might not have been the only man to go missing.'

Then, with the two men appearing reasonable, he

told them the story of how they'd been allocated the duty in the gully and how they'd found Baxter's body. The two men nodded frequently and maintained sombre expressions.

'A sad tale,' the first man said when they'd finished. 'Back in Ash Creek, Baxter and Peter joined up to work here at the same time as we did. We spoke a few times afterwards, but we haven't seen either of them this last week. It sounds as if Peter might be lying dead in the gully too.'

'And what did you find on him?' the second man asked.

Nathan winced. 'We don't actually have anything. We were just interested in finding someone who knew him.'

The two men considered this information then glanced at each other before the first man spoke up.

'We can't tell you much. Baxter and Peter worked hard and didn't come into town. All we know is they didn't have families and were just roaming from place to place looking for work.'

'They sound like us,' Jeff said with a sigh. 'But that makes us even more determined to find out what happened to them.'

'Then I wish you luck.'

Both men tipped their hats and moved to leave.

'Wait!' Nathan said, halting them. 'Who are you? In case we want to talk to you again.'

'If we learn anything, we'll find you.'

The men swung away and headed to the door with a determined tread.

'Why wouldn't they give their names?' Jeff asked as the men slipped outside.

'Two men have been killed for an unknown reason. I can't blame them for being cautious, but at least we have a couple of allies now and some extra information.'

Jeff nodded. Then, with greater hope, they resumed their questioning, but when they'd been around the rest of the customers that spark of enthusiasm had been quashed. Nobody else claimed to know of Baxter Meredith or Peter Parsons.

'Perhaps it's as those men said,' Jeff said when they'd left the saloon and were looking up and down the road wondering where to try next. 'Baxter and Peter had only just arrived. They didn't know anyone and they didn't talk to many people before they were killed.'

'Or maybe that's not the way it happened,' Nathan said. 'We don't know for sure that this Peter is dead, so maybe he's the one who killed Baxter. Then he left.'

Jeff shrugged and, deep in thought, both men trudged from the saloon and made their slow way past the station to the edge of town. As nobody was around they walked to the railroad tracks where they had a good view of the outcrop, its dark form blocking the stars.

57

'You reckon we'll ever get to it?' Jeff asked as they moseyed along beside the tracks.

'The nearer we get to the gold, the further away it seems, but. . . .' Nathan trailed off then shot Jeff a warning glance.

'What's wrong?' Jeff said using a normal voice, presumably having failed in the dark to pick up on Nathan's concern.

'I reckon,' Nathan whispered, 'we're being followed.'

Jeff cast his slow gaze along the tracks into the darkness.

'Then we'd better stay close to town, or we could end up dead in the gully too.' Jeff rolled his shoulders. 'On the count of the three, we turn and see who's interested in us.'

Nathan considered Jeff's smile, the teeth catching a stray beam of light.

'What you looking so pleased about?'

'Someone must have overheard us asking questions, and that's progress.'

Feeling cheered by Jeff's positive attitude Nathan whispered a countdown. Then both men swirled round with their fists bunched, but they faced only the darkened tracks leading on to the station.

'I heard someone,' Nathan said as they made their cautious way back. 'Perhaps more than one person.'

'I believe you,' Jeff said. 'They're here somewhere.'

They approached the town and the sounds of subdued revelry from the saloon they'd just left grew.

'But perhaps I don't trust myself. All this questioning has made me edgy. Perhaps I'm hearing things.'

Nathan expected Jeff to answer, but he said nothing and so Nathan turned, but Jeff wasn't beside him. He swirled round, but he wasn't behind him either. He started to snap out an urgent plea when footfalls pounded, moving away from the station.

He turned back as a man ran into him, knocking him to his knees. He looked up to see his assailant looming over him, his form a dark outline. Dangling from his right hand was a cudgel, which he proceeded to swing up.

Nathan jerked away, but the cudgel still caught him a glancing blow behind the ear that sent him sprawling. He landed on his chest then moved to get up, but his limbs refused to obey him and he slumped, his face pressed into the dirt.

It took a supreme effort to cling on to consciousness, but he must have failed as the next he knew he was being dragged across the ground. Then, seemingly moments later, he was lying propped up against a wall.

He sensed that someone was standing beside him and he tried to look that way, but his body wouldn't obey him. Through his swirling vision he saw Jeff lying on his back. Another man was going through his pockets.

Nathan gritted his teeth then tried to move towards them, but he succeeded only in rolling over on to his back. He stared up at the night sky where the stars winked out as his vision dimmed.

'What you two doing?' someone shouted, dragging him back to consciousness.

'Get away,' another man said. 'This don't concern you.'

'I reckon it does.'

Heavy footfalls sounded, then the thud of fist on flesh. Still unable to summon the strength to move, Nathan's head lolled to the side and with his cheek pressed against the dirt he watched the blurred forms of two men tangling with their two assailants.

Muttered comments and brief glimpses of their features in the low light tapped at his memory and convinced him that he'd seen two of the men before, but in his befuddled state he couldn't place where.

His eyes closed. Even with the altercation raging a few feet away sleep was close and inviting.

'Is he dead?' someone asked, the words seeming to come from miles away even though he knew the speaker stood nearby.

Then the words became too hard for him to concentrate on and sleep stole him away. Flashes of light and disconcerting movements interrupted a troubling sleep until he realized that the latest movement was someone shaking him. He pushed the hands away, but they wouldn't leave him alone and with a start he opened his eyes to find bright light shining down on him.

He blinked and raised an arm before his face to block the light, but quickly his vision focused. He was no longer outside. He was in the lawman's office.

'Are you all right?' Marshal Lawton said.

Nathan fingered his forehead, then around his head until he found the bump behind the ear. He flinched away from it wincing, but then probed again, finding that aside from being damp the wound wasn't as painful as he'd first feared.

'I guess,' he said.

He sat up. The motion made him sway, but once he'd righted himself he found he was sitting on the floor beside the desk where yesterday Lawton had given them an ultimatum. To his relief Jeff was propped up against the wall and although he too was fingering his scalp gingerly he summoned a smile.

'You had me worried,' Jeff said. 'You've been out for an hour.'

'And you had me worried.' Nathan thought back to the scraps of conversation he'd heard. 'I thought they'd killed you.'

'The only reason they didn't is down to our new friends, Mike Ripley and Daniel Smart. They saved us.'

'The men from the saloon?'

'Sure.'

'Then,' he said, leaning back against the wall and relaxing, 'I'm mighty pleased to finally learn the names of our new friends.'

CHAPTER 6

'So Peter Parsons is the other dead man,' Marshal Lawton said.

'We don't know that for sure,' Jeff said, 'but it's looking that way.'

'Either way, you had a lucky escape.' Lawton headed to the window to look out. 'I was told two men were being attacked. When I found you, Daniel and Mike had just chased your assailants away. So it's likely that what happened to Peter and Baxter is what nearly happened to you.'

While he gathered his thoughts Nathan looked at the cells. They weren't as occupied as they had been yesterday, so he was able to catch Patrick's eye and give him an encouraging smile.

'I can't add anything to that story.'

'What were you doing to get attacked in the first place?'

'We were doing whatever it took to get Patrick

released,' Nathan said, raising his voice so that Patrick could hear. 'We only learnt the little you now know, but we have a start.'

Lawton narrowed his eyes. 'I didn't mean our investigation. I mean your own private investigation.'

'I don't know what you mean.'

Lawton snorted then paced up to them. He looked both men up and down, taking his time.

'You left town, walking down the tracks towards the outcrop, the one place where you're not allowed to go. That makes me wonder if you're really working with Patrick to steal the payroll, after all.'

Nathan rubbed his head, wincing. 'If you're going to be that suspicious, you'd better lock us up because to get the answers you want we'll be heading to all the places nobody else goes.'

Lawton considered this excuse while frowning, but then accepted it with a brief nod.

'You've raised plenty of questions,' he said. 'So now find me some answers.'

It was pay day.

The miners had formed an orderly line behind a row of tables set in the centre of the tents. Sherman Clarke stood behind the central table eyeing the surrounding area as if he suspected someone would attempt a raid at any moment.

Standing to the side was Marshal Lawton. He kept far enough back from Sherman and his people to appear as if he were looking out for trouble without intruding on Sherman's area of responsibility. It didn't take long for his steady consideration of the miners to centre in on Nathan and Jeff.

Nathan shook his head, receiving a snort in response. In the three days since they'd last spoken to him, he and Jeff had made no headway in uncovering information about the missing men, nor were they any the wiser about who had attacked them.

With the work clearing the gully taking up most of their time, they had only the evenings in which to find out what they could. But they had been unable to put their few hours of free time to any use. The attitude they'd encountered had been the same as they'd received on their first night of investigating – the miners became suspicious when they mentioned the body they had found.

In the daytime Tucker and Clay worked with surprising diligence, but they weren't interested in working out what had happened to Baxter, so Nathan presumed they were carrying out their own plans to find the gold.

They hadn't come across Peter's body in the gully. Neither had they seen Daniel and Mike again.

That thought made Nathan look around for either twosome; none of them were visible despite the imminent paying, but he did notice that the miners were becoming more animated.

Everyone was craning their necks looking beyond

the circle of tents, and when Nathan moved over to see what had interested them he saw the procession of men coming down from the outcrop.

Two men were up front leading a wagon on which men sat at each of the corners. Two more men rode along behind. Several riders were further away taking in all the possible places from where an attack might come. These men were the first men he'd seen packing guns since the night at the outcrop, but presumably Lawton allowed Sherman's trusted workers to do so.

With much bustle they drew up between two tents at which stage two men transferred a crate on the back of the wagon to the ground. They formed a cordon around it with only a gap on the side facing the table through which Sherman entered then emerged a few moments later with a folded bundle.

When he'd positioned himself behind the main table the payment procedure got underway. With Nathan and Jeff being at the back both men looked around, wondering from which direction trouble might emerge, but as they slowly shuffled forward, Nathan couldn't see any hints of anything happening.

'It's hard to see why anyone would try anything,' Jeff said, matching Nathan's thoughts, 'with this much firepower and this many men guarding the money.'

Nathan nodded. Then they reverted to silence as

they made their slow way onwards. Closer to Nathan noted the careful scrutiny everyone was getting.

Every miner was quizzed about his identity, the questions usually being greeted with surly and short answers. The slow progress led to more men moving over to deal with the questioning, but the interrogations continued in an exhaustive manner.

After payment, the miner got a dab of paint on his hand. Each man wasted no time in shaking the hand and trying to wipe it away, but enough colour remained to ensure anyone attempting to get paid more than once would be spotted.

This process continued until Jeff and Nathan filed up to the table.

'Name?' Sherman asked.

'It's Nathan Palmer.'

Sherman looked him up and down, his sceptical gaze taking in his features as if he'd never seen him before, even though he'd been berating him for his tardiness only an hour earlier at the gully.

'It would appear you are. Sign here or put a cross.'

Nathan signed his name, after which he had a daub of the thick green paint slapped on the back of his hand.

'Are you always this careful?' he asked.

Sherman stopped counting out the money to lean back in his chair and peer up at him.

'Now why would that interest you?'

'No reason other than nobody seems happy with

these arrangements.'

Sherman considered him then apparently dismissed his concerns with a shake of the head and resumed counting out his money.

'I paid Baxter Meredith last week, except he was dead, and I paid Peter Parsons too even though nobody remembers seeing him recently. This week I'm making sure that everybody is who they say they are.'

Sherman held out the money and favoured him with a long look before he moved on to the next man and repeated the procedure.

Nathan walked down the line slowly, waiting for Jeff to catch up with him. As he looked along the line of miners, who were all craning their necks as they monitored progress, he noted two men at the back who weren't acting in such an animated manner.

Nathan smiled and hurried on to join them.

'I haven't seen you two since you helped us,' he said.

Mike broke off from his conversation with Daniel to consider him.

'We've been working long hours,' he said.

'Then I assume you haven't found out anything about Baxter or Peter?'

'Nope, but then again we haven't been looking.' Mike shrugged. 'We only talked with them on the way from Ash Creek, so we didn't know them well.'

'And it seems as if you were the only people who

knew them at all.'

'Perhaps, but why are you so interested in people you've never even met?'

Nathan smiled. 'It's more interesting than blowing up rocks.'

The two men accepted that explanation with snorts of laughter. Then they looked past Nathan to nod to Jeff as he approached.

'They seem to be checking everyone,' Daniel said.

'Yeah,' Jeff said raising his green hand. 'They're being thorough.'

Jeff went on to explain the procedure. The two men listened intently then looked at each other, suggesting they wanted to discuss something. After an awkward silence had dragged on for several seconds, Daniel spoke up.

'When we've been paid,' he said, 'perhaps we'll see you in the saloon.'

'I reckon that's a fine idea.'

Nathan relaxed as the suggestion captured his imagination. They had been suspicious and on edge ever since they'd arrived in Copper Town, so relaxing for once sounded a good idea. He looked beyond the line of men to see that Marshal Lawton was advancing on them.

Daniel and Mike saw him coming. They drew down their hats and shuffled forward in the line. Gathering that they weren't eager to meet the lawman, Nathan and Jeff peeled away from the queue to join him.

'I reckon it's too late for a raid,' Nathan said.

'It is,' Lawton said, noting the short line of miners who had yet to be paid. 'So now I'm more interested to see what Sherman's arrangements throw up.'

Nathan took a deep breath. 'We've not found out anything about Peter and Baxter.'

'I'd guessed you hadn't.' Lawton considered them. 'But if this payment goes through without a hitch, it'll take some of the tension away. A lot of new workers arrived recently and Sherman is suspicious of them all.'

'Not everyone who arrives looking for work is up to no good.'

Nathan glanced at Mike and Daniel, who were now approaching the tables. Lawton followed his gaze and provided a rueful snort.

'Perhaps not. People have many reasons for avoiding a lawman.' He sighed. 'But you have nothing to fear from me.'

Nathan considered Lawton's smile and his less belligerent posture than the last time they'd spoken.

'Does that mean you now accept that we're not up to no good?'

'I wouldn't go that far. I'll check out names once Sherman has a proven list, but if you haven't been lying, I don't reckon I'll be worrying about you again. I'd still be obliged if you'd tell me of anything you learn, but I won't hold the threat over you.'

Jeff and Nathan glanced at each other and smiled.

'And Patrick?'

'That's not up to me. He didn't do anything wrong other than to go into a restricted area. So it's up to Sherman whether he wants to keep him locked up.' Lawton looked down the short row, counting the number of men left to get paid. 'But once I've collected the wages for the men in my care, I'll ask Sherman what he wants to do about him.'

'Obliged.'

They stood in companionable silence as the queue dwindled. Nathan watched the payers gather and consult the list of names. They looked up at the men left to be paid then one man raised seven fingers.

'Five men are in my cells including Patrick,' Lawton said. 'So that means two more men are missing.'

As he moved to the tables, Nathan cast his mind back to the people he'd seen file up and he reckoned he knew who the two men who hadn't been paid were.

'Wait!' he called.

Lawton turned to him with his eyebrows raised, but as Nathan started to speak the reverberating boom of an explosion tore out. It was distant and although sounds of this nature were common, everyone in the queue flinched and looked around while Sherman and the rest behind the tables formed a defensive huddle.

71

Slowly everyone's gazes turned away from the mine and to the town, where a spreading cloud of smoke was rising.

'It's from the edge of town,' Lawton said. Then he winced, a hand rising to slap his forehead in shock. 'It's my law office. Someone's tried to blow up my law office.'

Lawton broke into a run heading to his horse. At his heels were Jeff and Nathan. As they ran Nathan glanced at Jeff to tell him what he'd considered, but Jeff had already worked it out.

'It's Tucker and Clay,' he said. 'They've used the dynamite to break Patrick out of jail.'

CHAPTER 7

On foot Nathan and Jeff reached town several minutes after Marshal Lawton.

When the main road came into view they saw that Lawton had been right. A spreading plume of smoke surrounded the law office. Several men were staggering away from the building with their hands to their heads while coughing. From within the circle of thick smoke, raised voices sounded.

Lawton's voice clearly gave an order and in confirmation of Nathan's and Jeff's assumption Clay shouted out a rough retort. The law office was still two hundred yards away when the wagon they'd used earlier in the week to transport water emerged from the smoke.

Riding up front was Tucker while Clay was in the back with Patrick. As Lawton ran out of the smoke in pursuit, Clay pushed Patrick to the base of the wagon and out of their view.

'Stop!' Lawton shouted, breaking into a run, but with a shake of the reins Tucker hurried the wagon on down the road.

Only a few other miners had followed them into town and they'd spread out to eye the aftermath of the explosion, leaving Nathan and Jeff as the only men standing before the speeding wagon.

With a glance at each other, both men agreed they'd try to stop it. They spread out.

Behind the wagon Lawton gave up on the chase and slowed to a halt then kicked at the dirt. So with this being their only chance of stopping Patrick's kidnap, they both waited in a position where they were as close to the path of the wagon as they dared.

Tucker glared down at them as he rode closer, but he still steered the wagon on a straight course between them.

The moment the horses had thundered by, Nathan leapt forward. He slapped a hand on the speeding wagon and ran along beside it, managing to match its speed for several paces before he leapt up.

He looped an ankle on the board and hung on with one arm and one leg dangling. Slowly he righted himself then dragged himself up and when he managed to rest his chest on the board he saw that Jeff had used the same manoeuvre, but Clay was trying to push him away.

Unable to fight him off Jeff was struggling to keep

hold, but that at least gave Nathan the freedom to clamber up. He swung his other leg up and caught the board with his ankle then rolled onwards to land on the base.

He landed heavily gathering Clay's attention, who with a grunt of anger thumped his fist down on Jeff's hand making it fall away. As a clatter sounded below as Jeff fell to the ground, he turned to him, but he was wringing his hand.

Nathan advanced on him and gave him a firm shove that rocked him back to the side of the wagon where he waved his arms as he struggled for balance. He righted himself with a hand on the back of the driver's seat then swung round to face him.

The barrels were at Nathan's back ensuring he couldn't be pushed over the back; Patrick sat propped up in the corner. The old-timer looked up at him with unfocused eyes that didn't appear to register that he recognized him.

Nathan put him from his mind and concentrated on Clay. He spread his arms and crouched while planting his feet firmly on the base of the wagon.

Clay considered his confident stance then muttered something to Tucker in the front. Tucker looked back to see the situation wasn't under control and then with an angry grunt to himself, veered the wagon around the last buildings and down to the rail tracks.

The sudden movement made Nathan sway to the

side, but Clay had anticipated the change of direction and he wasted no time in throwing himself forward. Nathan's back slammed into a barrel, but Clay continued to drive on making him flex backwards over the barrel rim.

His back protested and so he extricated himself by twisting to the side. That manoeuvre only let Clay get a firmer grip of his shoulders and push him down towards the barrel.

Clay slammed his head down, then again. Both times Nathan managed to get his arms up before his head and cushion the blow, but judging that one of the shoves was sure to work before long he reached back to grab him. Unfortunately, that gave Clay an opening and he slapped his forehead down with a jarring thud.

Momentarily stunned Nathan could do nothing to defend himself as Clay bundled him along beside the barrels. The hard ground beckoned below and a simple shove would send him over the edge.

In desperation Nathan lunged. His right arm flailed through the air, but his left hand clamped on the rim of the endmost barrel, so when Clay shoved him he managed to hang on and swing himself around it. He still careened towards the back of the wagon, but after two out of control paces he halted his motion with a firm grip of the final barrel.

He fetched up standing against the backboard and staring over the tops of the barrels at Clay, who considered him with surly confidence.

Then, with a roar, Clay kicked out, planting the sole of his boot against the nearest barrel. It was empty and toppled easily into the barrel behind it, which slammed into Nathan.

He jerked aside to put himself behind the second row of barrels, but Clay was already kicking that row while the first row had slammed against the backboard and tipped it down. The barrels went rolling over the edge to spill down on the ground and when the second row hit Nathan in the chest, he doubted he could do anything to stop himself joining them.

He landed on his side on the now horizontal backboard and moved to grab the edge, but hadn't quite reached it when a barrel came toppling down on him. In a cascade of rolling barrels he tumbled to the ground where he too went spinning end over end until he fetched up flat on his chest.

Gingerly he tried to rise. Then he wished he hadn't moved when the last barrel bounced on to his back and pressed his face down into the dirt. He gave up all thoughts of pursuit and lay still until Jeff joined him.

'You fine?' he asked.

'I will be,' Nathan said.

He let his friend help him up to a sitting position. Then both men rubbed their arms and legs locating bruises and wincing while they watched the wagon trundle over the rail tracks. When it'd disappeared from view they got to their feet then turned back towards town.

They hobbled along, taking considerably longer to cover the few hundred yards to the buildings than they had taken to leave them. Nathan expected that Marshal Lawton would pursue the wagon on horseback, but when they reached the main road instead he had rounded up the other prisoners and was directing them back to the jailhouse.

With the smoke having cleared, Nathan could see the large hole in the side wall that had clearly been made with dynamite purloined from the excavations in the gully. Through the hole the cells were visible, but they were intact, suggesting Lawton would still be able to function.

More miners had wandered away from the mine to join those watching the situation, although as they'd been paid and the work shift for many was over, there was a significant drifting towards the saloons.

When Lawton saw Nathan and Jeff he pushed the last man through the door, shouted a stern warning inside, then swung round to await their arrival.

'He doesn't look happy,' Jeff said.

'Can't blame him,' Nathan said. 'He's got a big hole in his jailhouse and a prisoner is free.'

'You might not blame him, but I reckon he might blame us.'

Nathan was about to disagree, but then he got close enough to see Lawton's blazing eyes.

78

'You've lost me a prisoner,' Lawton shouted.

Nathan spread his hands as they came to a halt before him.

'We tried our best.' He batted the dust from his clothes. 'But they beat us off.'

'I didn't mean that little disagreement you had back there. I mean that this sheds a whole new light on your activities. The two men you were working with just happened to break Patrick out of jail while your aimless chatter was distracting me.'

'We didn't know they were planning that, and besides I don't reckon they've exactly broken him out of jail for his own good.'

'Perhaps you're right. Perhaps it's all about a squabble between raiders, but I'm going to make my life easier by stopping your two's plans.' He glanced at the ruined jailhouse then offered a harsh smile. 'You can take Patrick's place.'

'But we haven't done nothing wrong.' Nathan watched Lawton point firmly at the jailhouse, but neither he nor Jeff moved. 'There must be something we can say to convince you we're innocent.'

'Nothing you can say will keep you out a cell.'

'Except,' a voice said from behind them, 'for the truth.'

Nathan turned to find that Mike and Daniel had arrived.

'The truth?' Nathan murmured, unsure what these men might reveal.

79

Daniel cast him an amused glance then walked by them to stand before Marshal Lawton.

'I'm guessing you're not sure whether these men are idiots, or whether they are men who are trying to look like idiots to cover up what they're really doing. Well, you were right the first time. They're idiots.'

Nathan opened his mouth to complain while moving forward, but Jeff grabbed his arm and drew him back then cast him a warning glance that said he should let Daniel have his say.

'How do you know this?' Lawton asked.

'We've been asking around. It seems they really did come to Copper Town to search for a gold seam. They're not up to no good. They're just misguided prospectors. Tucker and Clay spirited Patrick away to get him to tell them where the gold is, except of course there is no gold and so I guess some time soon you'll find a body.'

Lawton set his hands on his hips as he considered this tale. Slowly a smile spread across his lips. He faced Nathan and Jeff.

'You know,' he said, 'I believe that. You two being idiots fits the facts a lot better than you two being raiders.'

'It does,' Nathan said through gritted teeth while forcing himself to remain calm by gripping his hands into tight fists.

'So good luck with finding that gold!' Lawton threw back his head and laughed then waved a dismissive hand at them. He headed back to his ruined building, except this time he had a spring in his step.

Only when he'd disappeared from view did Daniel and Mike swing round to face them.

'Obliged, I guess,' Nathan said, with Jeff echoing his comment.

'No problem.' Daniel gestured to the nearest saloon. 'Now I reckon we need to talk.'

CHAPTER 8

'The whole story is a long one, but you have the basics,' Nathan said when they'd taken their whiskeys to a quiet table in a corner of the saloon where they'd first met Daniel and Mike.

'We thought so,' Daniel said, 'but that still leaves the big question. Clearly you believe the story and so do Tucker and Clay, but do we?'

Nathan spread his hands. 'That's for you to decide, but if it helps, we've never been sure whether to believe it ourselves.'

Jeff nodded. 'Yeah. At first we thought it a tall story, but we weren't doing anything important and so we came here. Either way, we now have work and we have some dollars in our pockets, so no matter what the truth is, it's not been a disaster.'

'But,' Mike said, 'you believed the story enough to try to save the old-timer.'

'We did, but we didn't do it for the gold,' Nathan

said. He glanced at Jeff, who frowned, acknowledging that even though they were avoiding telling the full story, bit by bit it was coming out. 'Marshal Lawton had us in a difficult position. He said he'd free Patrick and not arrest us if we found out why Baxter Meredith was killed.'

Daniel and Mike both let out long whistles then leaned back in their chairs. They glanced at each other and their small facial ticks appeared to indicate that this revelation helped to confirm their own theories.

Both men sipped their whiskeys and mulled things over before Daniel leaned back on the table.

'I'm glad you've been honest with us. We couldn't work out why you were concerned about the fate of two men you'd never met. So now we'll be honest with you. We've worked mines for more years than we care to remember and it's got us nowhere. We'd like to get our hands on this gold, but even if it's not here, we'd settle for enjoying the hope.'

Nathan nodded. 'We had the same conversation when we joined up with Patrick.'

Daniel fingered his whiskey glass then took a deep breath before in a low voice, he asked the question Nathan had been expecting.

'So where is this gold seam?'

Nathan rubbed his jaw. Clearly some of the information these men had heard was incorrect, and although Daniel and Mike were looking at him intently, Nathan turned to Jeff and raised his eye-brows. Jeff nodded and so Nathan spoke up, although he resolved to keep some information back.

'It's beyond the gully where we're blasting out rocks. The trouble is, we don't know exactly where.'

Daniel narrowed his eyes, conveying that he thought he was holding out on him.

'That's the truth,' Jeff added. 'Patrick explored there on his own, but Sherman thought he was searching for the payroll and had him arrested.'

Daniel nodded, this answer appearing to appease him.

'With everyone paid,' he mused, 'there's no money to guard until the next train arrives. The area should be free now.'

'That's our hope.'

'Which leaves us with the final big question.' Daniel merely smiled leaving Nathan to surmise it.

'If you hadn't stepped in the first time, we'd be dead. If you hadn't stepped in the second time, we'd be arrested. So I reckon we can strike a deal.'

While Daniel and Mike both nodded Jeff spoke up.

'Not that we need to worry about the details. We had a deal with Patrick, and we don't know for sure that there is any gold, so if we find any, that'll be the time to work out how we split it up.'

Mike snorted a laugh. 'That's the worst time to

84

decide. The sight of gold does strange things to a man. We decide now.'

'Patrick said the same.' Nathan sighed. 'But he's in a tough situation now, so I reckon he can't expect us to keep to the deal we originally had. I say we split whatever we find equally, including Patrick if he survives.'

Nathan and Jeff both held out their hands. After a round of shaking they refilled their glasses. Then they passed several minutes in pleasant silence until Daniel moved on to their plan.

'As Sherman might still be watching the outcrop,' he said, 'we shouldn't act tonight. So we start tomorrow and then we move quickly.'

'Why the hurry?' Jeff asked.

'Because,' Mike said, 'we have to find the gold before Tucker and Clay beat its location out of Patrick.'

The new day brought fresh hope that they might be able to get access to the outcrop, after all.

When they'd left the gully yesterday, it looked as if it'd take several more days to blast away the boulders. But overnight a landslide had cleared the top of the gully letting them see the outcrop and the cauldron before it.

The tunnels were in clear view and there was no sign of anyone being there. Sherman confirmed this when he joined them to survey the overnight movements.

'You're free to clear the gully today and then to go into the area beyond,' he said. 'It's no longer restricted.'

'Good,' Nathan said with a guarded tone as he'd noted the smirk hovering on Sherman's lips.

'That means you're free to find the gold and to keep it all for yourselves.' He mockingly hugged his arms to his chest parodying holding a valuable hoard. 'There's not much Lawton and I agree on, but we had a good laugh about that.'

'We're pleased you found it amusing, but it was Patrick who thought that. We've accepted he got it wrong and now we're just here to work, and we're doing a good job.'

'You were.' Sherman swung round to look at the main mine workings, drawing their attention to two men who were making their way towards them. 'But then half of your detail ran away to get rich with your friend. So you need more help.'

Nathan couldn't help but raise his eyebrows in surprise when two men came close enough for him to see that Daniel and Mike had been assigned to their detail.

'We're obliged for the help,' he said levelly.

'Don't be. This way I've got all the gold seekers in one place.'

Nathan and Jeff stayed quiet until the two men joined them, then had to grit their teeth as Sherman enjoyed himself pouring scorn on their dreams.

When he'd finished laughing at their expense the four men moved to begin work.

Sherman waited until they'd reached the nearest boulder then hailed them.

'What now?' Nathan snapped.

Sherman waved, signifying the gully then the area beyond.

'That landslide should let you finish up here today.' He licked his lips, relishing his next comment. 'So as soon as you're done, plant dynamite in the tunnels up there and open up the area. The outcrop is the next place we'll be mining. So you'd better hurry up and find your gold.'

Sherman roared with laughter, his voice echoing in the gully and providing a long refrain as he turned on his heel and headed back to the mine.

The four men watched him go. Then, with a series of irritated grunts, they turned back to consider the day's task.

'I reckon,' Daniel said, 'we'd all like to have the last laugh.'

His three colleagues murmured that they agreed before they got to work on a task that Nathan thought they wouldn't be able to complete that day. But as it turned out, within a few hours they'd cleared the gully.

Daniel and Mike were more knowledgeable than Tucker and Clay had been and so the precarious boulders blocking the gully needed only six well placed sticks of dynamite to bring them tumbling down to the bottom. Thankfully others would cart the rubble away now that they'd cleared a passage and reduced the boulders to manageable rocks.

They were able to walk relatively easily across the base and enter the cauldron for the first time. Daniel stayed outside to look out for anyone approaching while the others debated what they should do next.

They gathered at the bottom of the slope to look up at the tunnels and the stark and jagged rocks they would have to scale to reach them.

'This doesn't look promising,' Mike said, speaking for them all. 'We'll never find and mine a seam of gold in a day and still keep Sherman happy that we're laying dynamite.'

Nathan and Jeff were standing back; they shot each other a guilty glance. Mike and Daniel had done nothing but help them and yet they'd still kept secret one aspect of this quest, even though telling them what they were actually searching for wouldn't have compromised them.

'Perhaps we can't,' Nathan said, 'but what have we got to lose by looking?'

This positive thinking made Mike provide a firm nod.

'Agreed.' He pointed at the tunnels. 'You know more about the area than we do. So you explore the tunnels while we plant the dynamite.'

Nathan readily agreed to this plan, having thought

that it was more likely that their colleagues would volunteer to use their greater mining knowledge to explore the tunnels while he and Jeff laid the dynamite. But before they could get to work, Daniel returned shaking his head and pointing to the mine.

'Sherman's coming,' he said. 'That man doesn't miss anything.'

So they sat and awaited instructions, but if they'd expected praise for clearing the gully quickly, they'd have been disappointed. Sherman yelled at them for sitting around when there was work to be done and then he demanded that they finish the job straight away. When he'd finished Daniel stepped forward.

'You thought it'd take us all day to clear the gully,' he said, 'except we did it in a morning. And that's because now that those two good-for-nothing workers have gone, you've got people who know what they're doing.'

'You're blowing up rocks,' Sherman snapped with his hands on his hips. 'That's not exactly hard.'

'We don't just stick dynamite in the ground, light the fuse, then run away while hoping it'll do some damage. We work it out properly. We find the right cracks and flaws in the rocks.' Daniel gesticulated, miming placing a stick carefully into a crack. 'And then we—'

'How long?'

Daniel glanced at Nathan, his pensive gaze suggesting he was weighing up how much time he could buy them with this delaying tactic.

'I'd hope we could bring the whole rock face down in one by sundown.'

Sherman swung round to appraise the terrain while nodding.

'You have an hour,' he said. Then he walked off, picking his way through the gully.

'That's not long,' Nathan said, joining Daniel, 'but it's better than nothing. How long will it really take?'

'Fifteen minutes,' Daniel said. 'We'll get everything in place. Then we all start searching.'

After collecting the crate of remaining dynamite, they clambered up the slope. With the gully clear, the bulk of the mine rapidly came into view. The rest became visible when they reached the first tunnel where they paused to catch their breath.

Ahead was the ridge where a few days before they'd waited for Patrick to return. In the daylight Nathan could pick out an obvious trail that Patrick must have found. Sherman's form was visible heading back to the mine with a determined tread that left Nathan in no doubt he would return at the due time.

While Mike and Daniel agreed where they'd plant the sticks, Nathan and Jeff set about exploring the tunnels.

Deliberately Nathan chose the first tunnel in the line below the one Patrick had explored. But they didn't get far. A landslide had blocked the tunnel ten yards in and after experimentally patting the wall of rock and finding it solid they moved on to the next tunnel.

This one proved to be even harder to explore as it closed down after only a few feet. The next one continued for around twenty yards, but as the ground had fallen away a few feet in to create a sheer-sided hole, they didn't venture inside.

'Mike was right,' Jeff said. 'This doesn't look promising.'

Nathan glanced at Mike and Daniel to check they were out of earshot.

'Yeah. We'd better hope we can explore the proper one or we won't have enough time to find the nugget.'

With both men feeling gloomy about the situation, they moved on to the next row, where there were four tunnels. Patrick had explored the endmost one, so in keeping with their seemingly uninformed exploration they started at the opposite end.

This tunnel proved to be the most extensive so far, being shored up for thirty yards until a rock fall blocked the way. Even then there were gaps that could be explored.

They emerged then hurried on to explore the other tunnels. Luckily the next two had collapsed and so with a last glance at Daniel and Mike who were fussing over where they would lay the last batch of dynamite, they slipped into the final tunnel.

The entrance opened up on either side to present a natural cave. The actual mine tunnel started twenty feet away and the light cascading in through the entrance let Nathan see that it went on for some distance.

There were signs of habitation with scraps of discarded food, blankets and even a chair, confirming that the payroll had been kept and guarded here. They moved off to explore the tunnel, but they'd managed only a few paces when footfalls sounded behind them.

Nathan turned, expecting that Daniel and Mike had followed them inside, but the men who were approaching were doing so from the shadows.

The unmistakable sheen of gunmetal flashed a moment before the two men came into the full light.

'Tucker and Clay,' Nathan muttered.

'Yeah,' Tucker said, swinging his gun up to aim at him. 'Patrick talked, and that means we're getting to the gold first.'

CHAPTER 9

Following Tucker's instructions delivered at gun-point, Nathan and Jeff raised their hands then paced backwards to the wall.

'Lawton doesn't allow weapons,' Jeff said, eyeing the gun.

'We're leaving,' Tucker said, laughing. 'So we got our guns.'

'What happened to Patrick?' Nathan asked.

Their captors smirked, letting them think the worst before Clay pointed to the shadow-shrouded tunnel.

'He told us the truth to save his life,' he said. 'Now he's digging for his life.'

Tucker slipped to the side of the entrance and peered outside.

'Are those two the only ones here?' he asked.

'They are, although Sherman's due back soon.'

With Tucker looking outside and Clay guarding

them they stood in silence until Daniel called from outside.

'Anything interesting?' Daniel waited for an answer, but Clay clamped his fingers beside his lips telling them to be quiet. Daniel persisted. 'We've planted the dynamite. Do you want us to search in there or try another tunnel?'

The mention of dynamite made Clay flinch and Tucker turn away from the entrance.

'So that's what you were doing out there,' Tucker muttered, his tone accusing.

'Sherman didn't give us a choice,' Nathan said, 'but now that it's planted, we're all free to search for the nugget.'

'That's in hand. The only thing the rest of you will do is stay out of our way.' Tucker gestured outside. 'Get rid of them.'

Nathan cleared his throat before shouting.

'We've not found anything here, but the tunnel at the opposite end is deeper. Try there.'

Inside the tunnel both the captors and the captives held their breath.

'Then be quick,' Mike shouted. 'We're already using up the hour before Sherman returns.'

'Understood.'

Tucker placed his back to the wall beside the entrance and the gradual movement of his head marked Daniel's and Mike's progress, but then he winced.

94

'One of them is still coming here,' he muttered. 'Make him go away.'

Clay grabbed Nathan's arm and shoved him towards the entrance, but by the time he reached it Daniel was pacing up the last few feet.

'It's the one at the other end,' Nathan said, forcing a pleasant smile while pointing.

'I know,' Daniel said, 'but we need to compare tactics to make the best use of our time.'

Nathan kicked at the dirt as he searched for the right words to dissuade him. Nothing would come and worse, Mike had veered away from the other tunnel to approach him. He took a long pace outside.

'All right, we need to. . . .' Nathan trailed off when Daniel peered past him and Mike hurried closer. A feeling of inevitability overcame him.

'What's wrong?' Daniel asked. He waited for an answer, but when Nathan didn't reply, he moved to go by him.

Nathan made to block his way, but Mike side-stepped around his other side and when he lunged for his arm Daniel slipped by him. Then all he could do was turn and see both men stride into the tunnel then come to a halt, lower their heads, and with their hands raised move over to the side wall to join Jeff.

Clay stepped into view and beckoned him to join them.

'A warning would have helped,' Mike grumbled.

Nathan didn't meet his eye and instead faced their captors. He took a deep breath, searching for another solution, but he couldn't think of one other than to offer a compromise.

'Now we're all here we need to talk,' he said. 'Sherman wants this rock face blown up in less than an hour. That's not enough time to get the gold. The only way we'll get it is to work together.'

'And take equal shares,' Clay said, sneering, 'I suppose?'

Despite Clay's unpromising expression and Tucker's head shaking, Nathan smiled.

'A share of the gold is better than no gold.'

'No deal. There's too many of us now.' Clay gestured at the newcomers.

'We had no choice after you told them about the gold.'

'We didn't. We've never seen them before.' Clay turned to Tucker, who shook his head.

'We haven't,' he said. 'If there's any deals been done, they're your problem.'

'But that's not the truth though, is it?' Daniel said with quiet confidence. 'Jeff and Nathan didn't tell us nothing. So how else would we have found out you broke Patrick out of jail to make him tell you where the gold is?'

Tucker and Clay both shook their heads, but then at the same moment both men furrowed their brows. Slowly they turned to each other as it dawned on them that if they hadn't revealed the details, the other one must have.

'You fool,' Tucker muttered.

'You're the fool,' Clay snapped. 'I said nothing.'

Both men advanced a long pace on the other. Their eyes bored into each other, but with their attentions no longer on their captives, Jeff moved in.

He ran towards Tucker. A moment later Daniel reacted and leapt at Clay while Nathan and Mike both moved in.

Their captors broke off from their escalating confrontation and swung round to face the onslaught, but they were already too late. Jeff ran into Tucker and grabbed his gun hand. He pushed his arm up while Daniel did the opposite to the other man and went in low, grabbing Clay around the waist and pushing him backwards.

Clay backstepped twice before he stumbled and went sprawling on to his back. His gun hand hit the ground. He moved to raise it, but Nathan reached him and kicked out, the toe of his boot sending the weapon hurtling across the tunnel to slam into the wall.

Confident now of success, Daniel grabbed his vest front and hauled him to his feet. He stood him upright then delivered a round-armed punch that sent him staggering along towards Nathan, who repeated the action and sent him back to Daniel.

As they knocked him back and forth, Jeff kept

Tucker immobile while Mike joined him and reached up to prise the gun from his fingers. Then, with Mike holding the weapon on their opponent, Jeff turned Tucker round and shoved him against the wall, tearing the air from his lungs. He grabbed his shoulders and for his second shove he aimed to slam his forehead against the rock wall.

Tucker managed to cushion the blow with his fore-arms, but a second and a third shove proved too much for him and his head collided with a dull thud. As Jeff made sure he'd knocked the fight out of him with another thud, Nathan decided they'd handed out enough rough treatment to his and Daniel's opponent. With a firm kick to the rump he sent him tumbling out through the entrance.

The moment he'd passed by, Jeff released his hold of Tucker. The dazed man made two uncertain paces away, but that only brought him within range of Mike's boot and a second kick sent him after Clay.

Daniel gathered up Clay's gun then joined every-one in peering out through the entrance and watching the two men roll down the steep slope of the cauldron. They raised a trail of dust as with their arms and legs spread they went bouncing down to the bottom where they came to a halt spread-eagled on the ground.

The four men watched them, but they didn't move.

'Out cold, I reckon,' Daniel said.

'At the least,' Nathan said. 'But I reckon they deserve a broken leg or two.'

The others grunted that they agreed before they headed back into the tunnel.

'With that over with,' Mike said. 'I reckon it's time we shared everything that we know and decide how we're going to find this . . . this gold seam.'

Nathan noticed the hesitation, but before he could ponder on its meaning, rustling sounded behind him in the tunnel. He turned to see a faint light growing brighter as its carrier approached.

'Patrick,' Jeff said.

'I'm glad to see,' Mike said, 'that they brought him here.'

'Yeah,' Daniel said with laughter in his tone. 'He didn't deserve to get killed by those two after everything he'd been through.'

Mike joined him in laughing, the sounds reaching Patrick and making him stop twenty yards away while he was still in the shadows.

'Who's there?' he asked, putting a hand to his brow as he struggled to see when facing the brighter tunnel entrance.

Mike and Daniel took a backwards step into the shadows, an action which presumably encouraged them to speak up on their behalf. Nathan raised a hand.

'It's Nathan and Jeff along with two friends,' he said. 'Tucker and Clay won't give us any more trouble.'

'Who are your friends?' Patrick said, his tone sounding irritated that more people had become involved. He resumed walking, but he did so slowly with his head cocked on one side.

'Daniel and Mike. They saved our lives and they might well have saved yours too.'

'Then I'm—' Patrick emerged into full light. His gaze picked out the men by the wall.

For long moments nobody said anything as the two men looked at Patrick, who stared at them agog.

'How did you get out?' he murmured.

'We could ask you the same,' Daniel said.

'I served my time, but then again I did nothing wrong and you two—'

'Did nothing wrong other than get double-crossed by you.'

Daniel paced towards Patrick while Mike raised his gun.

'You people already know each other,' Nathan said.

Mike shot him a sneering glance, conveying how stupid the comment had been. From the determined way that Daniel was advancing it was also clear that their previous encounter hadn't gone well.

Patrick's gaze darted down to the guns. Then, without warning, he turned on his heel and hurried back into the darkness. His sudden action caught both men by surprise and as they didn't move Nathan set off after him.

100

Jeff had also had the same thought that this encounter would turn out badly, and he ran at his heels.

Daniel shouted at them to stop and one of them loosed off a shot that ricocheted off the walls before hurtling down the tunnel. Then Nathan slipped into the dark, his only guide being the bobbing circle of light ahead.

Ten yards on the light came to a halt and illuminated Patrick's face when he turned. He smiled on seeing them then ducked and edged forward, his motion letting Nathan see that he was slipping through a hole. Then he disappeared from view plunging the tunnel into darkness.

Slowly his eyes became accustomed to the low light, letting him see that they'd reached a rockfall with the hole being the only way forward. Then he made the mistake of looking back, dazzling himself with the light pouring in from the entrance, but Daniel's and Mike's forms were visible as they peered ahead.

Jeff grabbed his arm and drew him on.

'Come on,' he said. 'We need to move before they start shooting again.'

With Jeff guiding him by drawing his head down, he crawled through the hole to find they were in a small recess. Patrick was sitting to the side and out of view from the entrance. Nathan said nothing until Jeff joined him.

'Are we safe in here?' he asked.

'No,' Patrick said. 'But if they want to get us out, they'll have to come in and we can make it hard for them.'

'Agreed,' Jeff said, taking up a position on one side of the hole while Nathan took the other.

They waited for a minute for the men outside to make a move, but when they didn't come down the tunnel, Nathan sat back on his haunches and asked the obvious question.

'What's this argument about?'

'You can work it out, surely.' Patrick offered a smile that neither Nathan nor Jeff was prepared to return.

Nathan pondered, then provided his best guess.

'Those men were here with you fifteen years ago.'

'Yeah,' Patrick said with a rueful smile. 'They're Wallace Crowley and Foley Steele.'

'They told us they were Mike Ripley and Daniel Smart,' Jeff grumbled. He sighed. 'So who are Wallace and Foley?'

'Wallace found the nugget. Foley tried to help him get it out.' Patrick frowned. 'They failed, but this time they won't leave without it.'

CHAPTER 10

'Can you reach the gold?' Nathan asked.

Patrick frowned before he shuffled forward.

'I can reach it,' he said, 'if it's still there, but it'll take time. Can the story on why they're here wait until then?'

'It can,' Nathan said. 'But no longer. We need to know what we're in the middle of here.'

'In that case, hold them off, Jeff, while Nathan helps me on the last section.'

Jeff glanced at Nathan, who nodded before he returned a nod of his own.

'Just hurry back,' he said. 'They won't stay out there for ever.'

Patrick nodded then led Nathan to a thin gap beneath a fallen boulder. Nathan squirmed through the hole after him. When he emerged, he was pleased to see that the route ahead, although winding, could be traversed on hands and knees.

He crawled after Patrick. They'd rounded two bends before Patrick spoke up.

'Everything I told you was the truth. I just left out a few details.'

'I can accept that,' Nathan said, feeling a pang of guilt about his own recent attempts to keep secrets.

'But before I explain, remember what I told you: gold does something to a man. It can make friend turn against friend.'

'Mike . . . Foley Steele said that too.'

'He should know. Fifteen years ago, we got out of the tunnel, but in the rush to escape another landslide the gold got left back here.' Patrick pointed ahead into the darkness beyond the circle of light that his candle was casting. 'I tried to get it out, but Foley and Wallace wanted it for themselves. They killed everyone outside then waited for me to come out with the nugget.'

'What did you do?'

'I hadn't reached the gold when I heard the shooting, but I decided that getting out alive was more important. I sneaked away. They reckoned I'd found it and chased me, and they carried on chasing for the next six months until I fetched up in Ash Creek.'

'And then you got thrown in jail?'

Patrick came to a halt and shuffled round to sit and stretch while he waited for Nathan to join him.

'So you guessed that bit.' He sighed. 'After failing to get the gold, those two had gone from bad to worse. They raided the railroad payroll. When they got caught, they tried to buy some leniency by claiming I was an accomplice. I got thrown in jail for twelve years. They got longer terms, so they must have escaped.'

Nathan nodded, considering this tale, and although he couldn't be sure, it helped to clarify what he thought his recent colleagues had been doing since they'd come to Copper Town.

Foley and Wallace had arrived with Baxter Meredith and Peter Parsons, as they'd claimed, but they'd killed them and stolen their identities. They'd bided their time to reach the gold, but when Baxter's body had turned up, they'd lost their false identities.

They'd needed new ones and so they'd attacked them to take their names and to stop them investigating, but two innocent men had stepped in and saved them, Mike Ripley and Daniel Smart. They'd killed them instead. Then they'd resumed their plans to get the gold.

'I reckon they did.' Nathan gestured ahead. 'But let's see if we can find the gold first before we worry about their plans.'

'If it's all the same with you,' Patrick said, smiling, 'I won't go any further.'

Nathan peered past him, seeing a wall of rock at the furthest extent of his vision, but also several wide cracks that could be traversed with care.

'I can't find it alone. You need to keep going. This

situation looks hopeless, but there has to be a chance.'

'There is,' Patrick said. 'But as I said, the sight of gold does strange things to a man. Some men it turns bad, but in your case, I hope it'll make you inventive.'

'But you said you're not going any further. . . .' Nathan trailed off when he saw Patrick's smile. Then he noticed the bulge under the end of his jacket that he'd trailed out on the ground. He gulped. 'Are you saying what I think you're saying?'

'Sure am. I've found it. Prepare yourself.'

With his smile widening Patrick moved his jacket aside to reveal the lump beneath. If he'd been expecting a reaction, Nathan had no doubt he disappointed him.

The rock he revealed wasn't what he'd expected to see, although now that he saw it he wasn't sure what he had expected. Perhaps something that lit up the cramped tunnel with golden light and which appeared to be valuable enough for men to kill to get their hands on it.

Instead the rock was dust-coated and in the dim light it wasn't golden at all. It was a gnarled and pitted lump that had so many holes in it he presumed it was light. Although from the way Patrick then struggled to lift it on to his knees, it was clearly heavier than it looked.

Nathan reached out and brushed away a layer of dust. The rock was cool and touching it made it feel more real. He looked up to meet Patrick's eyes.

'I'm starting to feel inventive,' he said.

Patrick smiled. 'I'd hoped you would.'

He got to his knees and wrapped his jacket around the nugget then beckoned for Nathan to lead on back down the tunnel. With the light at his back and the growing light ahead, Nathan made quick progress. When he rolled out through the thin gap to join Jeff he wasted no time in giving a thumbs-up signal.

'Any change?' he whispered.

'Wallace and Foley are staying at the entrance. They've been talking quietly so I think they have a plan. . . .' Jeff trailed off when he saw Patrick roll into view then drag the bundle out after him.

He shuffled over to look at the rock, then to Nathan's amusement he reacted in the same non-plussed way.

'It's hard to believe we've been fighting over this, isn't it?' Patrick said.

Jeff touched the rock then stared at his fingertips, as if they might turn to gold.

'I guess I expected more,' he said.

'It'll look better in the full light. In here only experienced miners would recognize it for what it is. And that includes the men out there.' Patrick looked at Nathan with his eyebrows raised, asking him to outline his inventive idea.

As he didn't have one yet, Nathan merely smiled.

'Let me do the talking,' he said.

'Talk away,' Patrick said, gesturing to the hole.

Nathan shuffled to the side of the hole and sat with his back to the wall.

'You two out there,' he called. 'We need to talk.'

'There's nothing to talk about,' Foley said from some distance away.

'There is. This stand-off has to end within the next forty-five minutes.'

'We're armed. You're not. We don't have a stand-off.'

'We do. We're near the gold. You're not.'

'Gold can make you rich, but a gun can make you dead.'

Nathan didn't reply immediately, giving the impression he was thinking.

'The moment you try to come in, we'll disarm you. So we're safe in here.'

'For forty-five minutes you are. Then Sherman will return and the situation will get, shall we say, complex.' Foley laughed.

Nathan returned a snort of laughter. 'For that time you're safe too. Patrick's in the tunnel searching. If he gets back before our time is up, we can talk. If he doesn't, none of us get the gold.'

He waited for a reply, but other than Foley and Wallace muttering to each other, he heard nothing and so he deemed that the opening taunts were complete.

'What's this deadline?' Patrick whispered.

In hushed tones Nathan relayed the situation outside with the no-nonsense Sherman due to return to monitor progress. This news made Patrick smile.

'Why are you so pleased about that?' Jeff asked.

'A deadline concentrates the mind,' Patrick said, 'and when there's gold at stake, it might give us an opening.'

With that hope being the extent of Nathan's plans too, the three men settled down to await developments. They did their best to judge the passage of time. As the enclosed tunnel provided no stimuli, this wasn't easy, but as it turned out the men outside helped them.

'Thirty minutes before Sherman returns,' Foley called out presently. 'Any news in there?'

The three men glanced at each other and smiled, noting that they had broken the silence, suggesting they were getting nervous.

'Patrick's still searching,' Nathan called. 'He's found a way to the end of the tunnel, but it's hard to negotiate. Tucker and Clay didn't bring his tools. It'd help if you—'

'No. We're not leaving here on no errands.'

Nathan shrugged as his attempt to split them up failed, but when they settled down, they did so in a more contented mood, their confidence growing as the men outside became more agitated.

Foley paced up and down the tunnel, his travels

coming closer to their hole while Wallace stayed at the entrance looking out, presumably awaiting Sherman's return. Foley called out when twenty minutes were left, then called out at five minutes intervals, but if the countdown was meant to worry them it failed as his voice became more strained every time he spoke.

The ten-minute deadline had passed when Nathan gathered the others closer.

'Now's the time to act,' he whispered.

'They'll be more worried in another five minutes,' Patrick said.

'They will, but we need to get away too.'

'Agreed,' Patrick said.

Nathan swung round to kneel beside the hole. He still hadn't formulated a plan that he was confident would work, so his only hope was to create a situation then seize any opportunity that came along.

He took the bundle off Patrick and deposited it on the ground before the hole.

'Let's hope for some luck,' he whispered. Then he raised his voice. 'You two, Patrick is coming back down the tunnel.'

'Has he got the gold?' Foley said, coming closer.

Nathan caught the desperation and tension in his voice.

'Wait a minute. . . .'

Footfalls sounded as Wallace came over from the entrance and joined Foley.

110

'Come on!' Wallace muttered. 'Has he got it or not?'

'Patience. He's coming out now. He has something with him.'

Patrick obliged by grunting then crawling across the tunnel.

'Is it the gold?' Wallace asked.

Nathan looked out through the hole to see that the two men had stopped three paces away and were bending over to peer through the hole.

'It is,' Nathan said, putting a suitable amount of awe into his tone before he moved back out of view.

'Show us.'

Nathan opened the rolled-up jacket to expose some of the nugget. Then he placed it on the bottom of the hole. Sharp intakes of breath sounded.

'Step away and you'll live.'

'We'd prefer a different deal,' Nathan said, moving the bundle away.

'It's the only deal you'll get unless you want to start dodging lead.'

Nathan gnawed on his lip searching for an angle that might give them a chance. Then, in a sudden decision, he put the bundle down and shrugged out of his jacket.

He scooped up a rock that was broadly the same size as the nugget and wrapped it in his jacket. Then he placed the new bundle on the ledge, an object that in the low light should look the same as the other one had.

'In that case I'll bring it out,' he said. He laid a hand on his jacket as if he were reluctant to let the contents out of his grasp.

'Just leave it there,' Foley said.

Nathan ignored him. He pushed the bundle to the side of the hole then ducked to slip through. On the other side he straightened then clutched the rock to his chest.

Jeff quickly followed him out and stood to his side while Patrick held his hands out through the hole.

'Any tricks and I'll take it back,' Patrick said. 'Then I'll make sure you never find it.'

'We won't trick you,' Wallace said, keeping his gun trained on them. 'All we want is the gold. Hand it over and we'll leave.'

Nathan considered his opponents. Wallace had his back to the wall and Foley stood in the middle of the tunnel. Both men were being cautious and they would be able to deal easily with any duplicity. Despite that, the only action Nathan could think of was to play out his trick and see where it led.

He lowered himself to one knee, then held out the bundle. Both men leaned forward in eagerness giving him hope that he might catch them off-guard.

He took a deep breath before he placed the rock on the ground, but before he could raise his hands from it, a voice spoke up from behind them.

'Don't leave it there. Bring it to me.'

Nathan looked past Foley to see Tucker standing in the entrance. He was rubbing his forehead and he stood awkwardly as if he had yet to recover from the fall down the slope. Foley swung round to consider him, then sneered.

'You're unarmed, Tucker. You don't give the orders here.'

'I do,' Tucker said, smirking. 'Clay's found the dynamite. If we don't get the gold, he'll blow you all to hell.'

CHAPTER 11

While Foley backed away to the wall to join Wallace, Nathan clutched the bundle to his chest then stood and joined Jeff. Patrick stayed on the other side of the hole with the real nugget.

'If Clay lights the fuse, he'll kill you too,' Foley said, raising his gun to sight Tucker's chest.

Tucker rubbed his jaw ruefully, presumably remembering the beating he'd suffered.

'He won't. We've cut the fuses so they're just long enough for us to get away.' Tucker laughed then flexed a leg. 'After all, we know how long it takes to get down to the bottom of the slope. So, do we see if you can be as fast as we were, or do we get the gold?'

Foley glanced at Nathan, clearly judging how long it'd take to wrest the gold off him and run to the entrance, but Nathan pre-empted his decision by setting off walking down the tunnel.

'Stop!' Foley muttered.

'Let me do this,' Nathan said. 'Then we can all take our chances.'

Foley narrowed his eyes, but then he flashed a smile, acknowledging that he had understood Nathan's warning that he was planning something. He stepped aside and Nathan carried on past him.

'Keep on moving,' Tucker said from the entrance.

Pace by pace Nathan approached him. He was ten paces away and around the same distance from the back of the tunnel when Foley spoke up.

'No further,' he said.

As he'd planned to stop before he reached Tucker, Nathan did as ordered.

Tucker considered the armed Foley and Wallace at the back of the tunnel. Then, with a short gesture to Clay outside, he took three slow paces into the tunnel.

'Put it down then back away,' he said with an audible gulp that revealed the tension he was feeling.

Nathan followed the orders, placing the bundle at his feet then taking a pace backwards. Tucker signified that he should get further away and so he backed away to the wall where he could see both the entrance and the far end of the tunnel.

Tucker shuffled towards the bundle while darting his gaze from man to man, looking out for duplicity. Closer to he crouched and thrust out his hands ready to scoop up the rock then run.

Slowly his questing fingertips closed on a trailing

sleeve. Then, with a roll of his shoulders that gathered his confidence, he slapped a hand on the top.

Nobody else moved as he exhaled noisily. Then he swung back the top layer of the jacket to reveal the rock beneath. He moved to lift it out of the jacket, but then he stopped and peered at the smooth rock.

'I've never seen a gold nugget before,' he murmured, 'but this doesn't look like one to me.'

'It's not,' Foley muttered, moving off down the tunnel.

'What kind of trick is this?' Tucker stood while still peering at the rock in bemusement.

Foley continued to advance, but then a cry of alarm went up. Nathan turned to see that Jeff had taken advantage of the distraction to jump Wallace. He'd grabbed his gun hand and had thrust it high.

Foley slid to a halt and peered one way then the other, unsure which problem to deal with first, but Tucker had no problem in making his decision. He hurried to the entrance.

'It's a trap, Clay,' he shouted.

With Tucker slipping out of his sight, Nathan hurried to the rock then hurled it at Foley. The rock was heavy and he couldn't give it much momentum. It looped up in the air on a trajectory that would fall short.

Foley still flinched away, but even before the rock had dropped short of his boots Nathan was running towards him. With alarming speed Foley got his wits

116

about him and while side-stepping away from the rolling rock he trained his gun on him.

'What did you do with the gold?' he demanded.

Nathan slid to a halt four feet from him and seeing no choice, he raised his hands.

'The gold?' Nathan murmured, playing for time.

Down the tunnel Jeff was still struggling with Wallace and Patrick was peering out through the hole. Then a cry went up from outside the tunnel that concentrated all their thoughts.

'You shouldn't have played us for fools,' Tucker shouted. 'The fuses are lit. You're all dead men!'

While still keeping his gun on Nathan, Foley looked down the tunnel at Jeff and Wallace who had both gone rigid, their tussle forgotten.

'How long?' Nathan snapped.

'We gave ourselves two minutes to get away,' Foley said, his tone no longer confrontational, 'but if Clay's shortened the fuses. . . .'

Foley left the thought uncompleted, but his sudden sprint towards the entrance provided all the answers Nathan needed. Wallace tore himself away from Jeff's grip then set off after him.

On the run he cast Nathan a rueful glare and swung his gun towards him, making Nathan turn and double-over in a desperate attempt to avoid the shot, but he didn't fire.

When Nathan looked up Wallace had joined Foley in the entrance and was staring down the slope in frozen horror. While Wallace looked for a way down, Foley leapt forward. He went tumbling down the slope in the same manner as Tucker and Clay had done earlier. Wallace left in a more cautious manner.

Nathan waved overhead. 'Hurry up, you two. It'll blow at any moment!'

Jeff had already set off, but then skidded to a halt and hurried back to help Patrick out through the hole. The bundle containing the real gold nugget was thrust under an arm.

'I've got it!' Patrick shouted as Jeff grabbed his free arm and hurried him down the tunnel.

'Let's hope we get to enjoy it,' Nathan said as he broke into a run, 'for longer than the next five seconds.'

'We will,' Patrick said as he pounded along. 'Go left and get behind the boulder twenty yards away. That'll protect us.'

'But you don't know where they planted the dynamite,' Jeff said.

Patrick merely shrugged and so they all concentrated on running. Nathan reached the entrance and glanced down.

Clay and Tucker had already reached the bottom and were scurrying into the gully. Wallace wasn't in view while Foley was skidding down the slope on his back. He couldn't see the dynamite nor any sign of lit fuses, but he judged that as a bad sign. He turned to the left.

The huge boulder did appear big enough to protect them, but it was also further away than the twenty yards Patrick had promised. With a sinking feeling in his guts Nathan set off.

At every pace he expected the explosion, but he halved the distance in a few seconds without mishap. He glanced over his shoulder. Patrick and Jeff were at his heels, Patrick having sensibly handed the heavy rock to Jeff.

With his friends having as much chance of survival as he had, Nathan put his head down and sprinted. He pounded over the sloping ground, aiming for the highest side of the boulder.

On the run he reached the side, clambered over loose rocks, then threw himself to the ground. He rolled twice fetching up on his side behind the sheer mass of the boulder. He breathed a sigh of relief then moved to hurry the others into safety with him.

Patrick emerged around the corner first with relief etched into his face. Then Jeff appeared, looking over his shoulder. Nathan presumed he was worried about the imminent explosion and he shouted at him to hurry up, but then Wallace appeared at his heels.

Wallace leapt on his back, one hand clawing at Jeff's face, the other reaching for the gold. . . .

A deafening roar sounded.

The next Nathan knew he was lying on his back. His ears were ringing and a great weight was pressing down on his chest. He looked down expecting that something had landed on him, but there was nothing there.

He tried to sit up, but instead he succeeded only in rolling over on to his side. He lay, bemused and shocked, but he still felt as if a weight was on him.

A distracted part of his mind put the feeling down to numbness after the blast. Dust swirled then parted to let him see Patrick shuffling along, bent over.

'I'm here,' Nathan croaked.

Patrick carried on along the same path and disappeared from view.

Nathan took a deep breath and again tried to move. This time he rolled to his knees where he gathered his breath before standing and following Patrick.

He found him shuffling in a circle. He shouted his name twice without him hearing him. Only when he slapped a hand on his shoulder did he turn.

Patrick said something, but Nathan couldn't hear it, so he patted the side of his head. With a pop, his hearing returned.

'I can't find him,' Patrick was saying.

Nathan smiled. Now that he'd got his hearing back he could hear Jeff calling out from probably only a few yards away.

'Your hearing's gone,' he said, turning him in the direction of Jeff's calling and giving him a push.

'What?' Patrick said, as Nathan moved him on

through the dust. Only when the dim form of Jeff came into view did he hurry on to join him.

'We survived,' Jeff said, feeling his arms and legs as if he hardly believed it himself.

'And I can hear now,' Patrick said, receiving a relieved grunt from Nathan. He looked around. 'But where's the gold?'

The relief on everyone's faces at having survived the explosion fled.

They all looked around at the ground until Jeff turned on his heel and hurried out of view. They followed him until they found him stood over the broken form of Wallace, his limbs bent at awkward angles.

'He saved my life,' he said, 'not that he'd planned to.'

He knelt and rolled his body aside to reveal Nathan's rolled-up jacket.

'At least,' Patrick said, 'he got his hands on the gold before he died.'

They gathered around as he opened the jacket to prove they did actually have the nugget. Then they treated each other to a round of backslaps before turning their minds to what they did next.

The dust was clearing, letting them see the boulder that had protected them. Patrick directed them to go in the other direction.

Nathan and Jeff stood back to let him lead and he picked a route along the slope that would presumably get them to the ridge, although that remained out of sight.

Nathan heard nothing other than their feet crunching on the rock making him feel that they were the only ones to have survived the explosion, and when they reached the ridge and he looked back, that seemed likely.

The dust cloud had dissipated enough to let him see a devastating scene that made him gulp.

Beyond the boulder none of the tunnels had survived. The former outcrop was now a flattened area, the mass of rock having slid down into the cauldron where it would provide work for the miners for some time to come.

It was hard to believe anyone below could have survived. But most shocking was the boulder, which hung over a precipice with the ground having fallen away around it leaving just the small area where they'd hid.

'Lucky,' Jeff said, joining him in looking back.

'I prefer to think,' Patrick said, 'that I used good judgement in directing us there.'

Both men smiled then invited him to lead on down the ridge.

'Let's hope that luck holds out some more,' Nathan said as he slipped over the top.

'I reckon we've used up all our luck,' Jeff said. 'I'd prefer a good plan.'

'In that case,' Patrick said, 'we retrieve our horses.

Then we get out of here, unless you're minded to continue being miners.'

'We've had enough of that,' Jeff said. 'Now it's time to enjoy being rich.'

With everyone agreeing with that sentiment, they clambered down the ridge. They reached the flattened area in a few minutes then carried on down the railtracks towards Copper Town.

Ahead a commotion was in progress. Nathan presumed it was as a result of the explosion, but when they were closer to the station he saw that a train had arrived.

New workers had stepped out on to the short platform and they were looking up at the former outcrop where the spreading cloud now masked the devastation. Sherman was on the platform overseeing the process of booking them in, so he wouldn't be investigating the outcrop for a while.

Confident now that they should be able to reach their horses then slip away unseen, they left the tracks to head for the mine. They'd covered only fifty yards when Patrick grunted with irritation then drew them to a halt.

'What's wrong?' Jeff asked.

Patrick pointed, drawing their attention to a man standing between them and the mine: Foley Steele.

Worse, Foley had already seen them and was now walking purposefully on, his gun drawn and held low.

CHAPTER 12

The three men hurried back to the railtracks.

With the route to the mine blocked, they had no choice but to seek refuge in Copper Town. The diversion at the station was still ongoing and so they slipped past the train and reached the buildings without drawing attention upon themselves.

Not that anyone should have been bothered about them, as aside from carrying the large bundle they weren't doing anything to concern anyone. At the saloon where they'd first met Wallace and Foley, they looked back. Foley was advancing on them, maintaining a determined pace that would reach them in no time.

'Where?' Jeff asked, looking around the town, which in early afternoon was deserted other than the people congregating at the station.

Patrick looked to the station, suggesting he'd made the same observation.

'This way,' he said, gesturing, and without complaint they hurried around the side of the saloon and back to the station.

They approached the platform along the tracks. The back of the final car of the three that had drawn up partially hid them from the newcomers and the miners who were processing them. So when they reached the car they slipped around its side and stood with their backs to it.

To their left was the outcrop and to their right was another set of tracks used to turn the engine for its return journey to Ash Creek. Ahead there was nothing but the slope down on to plains. They'd climbed up the slope the week before when they'd first arrived and from memory there were no obvious places to hole up until they reached the river several miles on.

Nathan risked peering around the corner, then jerked back. Foley was striding around the corner of the saloon a hundred yards away. So they edged along then slipped into the gap between the cars to face the platform.

The queue was working its slow way onwards. Foley would reach them in seconds, but at least thirty people were around so they could mill in with them and perhaps hide.

Patrick had been looking the other way and with a grunt of alarm he grabbed his shoulder and drew him back.

'We can't try it,' he said.

'We have to,' Nathan said. 'And besides, Foley won't try anything while we're amongst so many people. We can stay with them, speak to Sherman, and then. . . .'

Nathan trailed off on seeing that Patrick was shaking his head.

'I'm not worried about Foley. It's the others.' He pointed out of town. 'Tucker and Clay survived the blast too, and they're heading this way.'

'Trapped,' Jeff murmured unhappily. 'We'll never reach the mine and our horses now.'

As Nathan nodded, from ahead the engineer called out to check everyone had disembarked. This made Patrick twitch as if a sudden thought had hit him. Then his gaze turned to the end car.

'There is one way out of this,' he said.

Nathan glanced at the car. 'We can hide in there for a while, but they'll find us eventually.'

'Perhaps.' Patrick winked, then took the bundle from Jeff and slapped it against Nathan's chest. 'Get on board and hide it. Then keep your head down while me and Jeff organize a little surprise.'

Nathan didn't wait for an explanation and did as told. He clambered over the couplings then up the steps to the door. He ducked down and slipped inside then picked a bench where he could look out on to the platform while still keeping hidden.

With the nugget tucked under the bench, he

126

looked for their pursuers but none of them was visible. A few clangs and subdued thuds sounded. Then Jeff and Patrick slipped through the door and scurried along to join him.

'Finished?' Nathan asked.

'We just have to wait,' Patrick said, smiling, 'and our escape will be complete.'

Outside the engineer again called out, making Nathan shake his head.

'You're not planning for us to leave on the train, are you?' he asked.

'Not exactly,' Patrick said.

Nathan started to ask for more details, but Patrick put a finger to his lips, so the three men shuffled down beside a window where they'd be out of view of anyone looking in.

With bated breath, they awaited developments. They didn't have to wait long.

'What are you doing here?' Sherman Clarke intoned from a position a few windows along.

'We blew up the outcrop,' Foley Steele said. 'But the rest decided they'd done enough for the day and came back here. I need to find them.'

Sherman grunted, Foley having picked the right thing to say to get his attention. Then footfalls sounded, getting closer to their car. Inside, the three men cast pensive glances at the door.

The train lurched, shunting the cars against each other. Then they moved steadily backwards.

'If they're going to search,' Nathan said, 'they'll have to do it quickly.'

'They might not,' Patrick said. 'The engineer is only moving the engine back into the sidings to take on water and to turn it round for the trip back later. The train is going nowhere.'

'How do you know this?'

'I talked to the miners back in the jailhouse.'

Nathan blew out his cheeks in bemusement. 'It must have been boring in there if that's what you talked about.'

Jeff chuckled and cast an amused glance at Patrick, suggesting he knew the full plan, but Nathan resisted the urge to ask what it was as the cars clanged together then were shunted backwards. Nathan relaxed as it was unlikely that anyone would search the cars while they were moving.

They'd moved on for a few dozen yards when a cry of alarm went up from the platform that made Patrick smile. Then the clanging of the cars and engine stopped, but Nathan's limited view of the roofs showed that they were still moving backwards. It was only at a walking pace, but they did appear to be speeding up.

'It's working,' Patrick whispered, as if he didn't want to jinx his plan by speaking loudly.

'What's working?' Nathan said. 'We're still being shunted backwards.'

'We're not,' Jeff said, raising himself to look at the

station. 'We uncoupled us from the next car.'

'Why?' Nathan said. 'That'll just make sure someone searches in here.'

'Only if they can catch us.' Patrick joined Jeff in raising himself to look through the window. What he saw made him pat Jeff on the back.

Nathan joined them to see the station slowly receding. They were already closing on the outskirts of town.

People were moving towards their car, but in a bemused way with their hands on their hips. Foley and the rest of their pursuers weren't in sight.

'Is someone going to tell me what's happening?' Nathan said.

'We're leaving town,' Patrick said.

'Backwards,' Jeff added with an incredulous raising of his eyebrows as if he didn't believe it himself.

Nathan recalled that the tracks were on a slight slope. A free car given momentum by being shunted into by the engine could be easily sent on its way.

'We won't be riding a runaway car all the way to Ash Creek,' he said, 'so what do we do when it stops?'

Patrick rubbed his jaw while biting his bottom lip.

'It won't get us that far, but it's getting us out of town unseen. We wouldn't have got away from the people looking for us, so this is the only option I could see.'

Nathan accepted this explanation with a nod as he

watched the last building drift by. They were now moving at a fast walking pace. When he pressed his face to the glass, he couldn't see anyone coming after the car.

He went to the door at the front and glanced through the small barred window. The distant figures at the station were congregating to discuss the situation and the engine had stopped moving.

'Did the miners who gave you this idea say how far the slope goes on for?' he asked, turning back to face the others.

Patrick winced then shuffled round to sit on a bench. He dragged the rolled-up jacket out from under the bench and unwrapped it. The sight of the gold in full light made him sigh with relief and then, seemingly emboldened, he looked up.

'Apparently this happened accidentally last month. The couplings came apart and the end car went trundling off down the tracks. It was too dangerous to try to stop it, so it went faster and faster until it disappeared out of town. Sherman was annoyed about it, so I guess he'll be even more annoyed this time.'

Jeff nodded happily and settled down on the bench beside Patrick to consider the gold at their feet, but Nathan had noticed Patrick's pensive expression and tone. He paced down the aisle towards him.

'That didn't answer my question,' he said, lowering

his voice.

Patrick cast him a quick glance then returned to looking at the gold.

'The car kept going for some miles, perhaps even a quarter of the way back to Ash Creek. . . .'

'That still leaves a long way to go,' Jeff said. 'We'll never reach Ash Creek afoot.'

Patrick shrugged, not meeting either man's eyes.

'I don't reckon,' Nathan said, 'that's the problem, is it, Patrick?'

Patrick gave a barely perceptible nod. 'The car kept going until it reached this place called Devil's Bend. By then it was going so fast it came off the tracks and smashed to pieces.'

Jeff swirled round to look at him.

'You never told me that when you asked me to remove the coupling.'

As Patrick and Jeff snapped comments at each other, both men raising their voices and talking over each other as their anger grew, Nathan looked outside. The terrain was now moving by at a speed he would struggle to achieve on foot.

He went to what was now the front window to look down the track at the route they would follow, it was straight with the slope being shallow enough to suggest they wouldn't speed up much yet. The land on either side was barren.

'This wouldn't have been my first choice for a way to escape,' he said silencing the two men, 'but it might work. We stay on board until we're out of town. Then, before we reach Devil's Bend, we find somewhere soft to jump off. Then we return to Copper Town at night, find our horses, and leave.'

Jeff slapped his hands together with a determined clap.

'That sounds like a plan to me,' he said.

'And so,' Patrick said, 'come over here and enjoy the sight of what this has all been about.'

Nathan hurried down the aisle to the other door to check nobody was pursuing them. Then he did as suggested and sat on the bench opposite Patrick where he relaxed for the first time in a while.

They still had plenty of problems to resolve, but the gold nugget looked more appealing now and he could imagine it really would change their lives for the better. After drinking in his fill, he shuffled along the bench and looked out the window.

For the next hour the car never went faster than a gallop and on flat stretches it slowed down to a fast canter before again picking up speed. So it wasn't hard for Nathan to believe they were on a normal train journey and not on a runaway car that was hurtling to its destruction.

When he judged that they were around twenty miles out of town, the terrain changed. The river from which they'd collected water swung round to run alongside the tracks. But it was a hundred feet below and faster-flowing than further upriver.

Nathan peered out of the windows on every side.

'It's getting more rugged out there. I reckon Devil's Bend must be close.'

As if to confirm his thoughts, the timbre of the car's trundling over the tracks changed in rhythm and he was sure the terrain was noticeably passing by more quickly.

'We need to jump off the first chance we get,' Patrick said, joining him.

Nathan nodded and while Jeff folded his jacket around the nugget, he headed down the aisle to the door. The slope ahead was the steepest he'd seen. Even more worrying the tracks were swinging towards the river on the start of a long curve.

Judging that this was the time to get off, he pushed the door, but then slammed into it.

He shook himself, then tried the door again, confirming to his irritation that it was locked. Patrick and Jeff smiled at his discomfort as he headed back down the aisle to the door through which they'd entered.

He pushed, but the same thing happened again. The second door was locked too.

They were trapped inside. And they were speeding up with every passing moment.

CHAPTER 13

'Both doors are locked,' Nathan said, swirling round to face the others.

'They can't be,' Patrick said, hurrying past him.

Nathan stood aside to let him try, but Patrick also failed to budge the door, as did the burlier Jeff.

'It can't be locked,' Patrick said, tipping back his hat. 'We came in this way.'

'And yet,' Nathan said as Jeff gave up on trying the handle and put a solid shoulder to the door, again without success, 'the door won't move.'

'It must have locked itself.'

Jeff tried again then turned to them.

'Stop worrying about how it happened,' he said, 'and just work out how we get out of here.'

Nathan looked around the car for something they could use to batter down the door. He experimentally kicked a bench but it was bolted down. Then his gaze alighted on the gold nugget.

He smiled. 'The nugget was supposed to change our lives, but perhaps it can save them.'

Jeff nodded, then hurried past him to gather it up. When he reached the door, he glanced at Patrick, who stood back nodding.

Jeff rolled his shoulders. Then he crunched the sharpest end of the nugget against the wood beside the handle. It hit with a dull thud, so he swung back his arm for the second attempt, but he didn't follow through.

'Do it,' Patrick said. 'It won't matter if you knock bits off.'

'It'll matter to us,' a voice said from beyond the door. Then Tucker stepped into view on the other side of the glass. Clay was at his side.

'How did you two reach us?' Jeff murmured, backing away for a pace.

'We got on board the car at the station, except we can leave it when we want to and you can't.' Tucker hammered a fist on the door to emphasize his point. 'We've barred the door. You'll never break it down.'

Nathan stepped up to the door and looked down. He could see the solid beam they'd placed across the doorway, and the barred window was too small to climb through.

'So what's the deal?' Nathan asked, spreading his hands and putting on a pleasant smile.

'There isn't one. We heard the tales about the car that got loose last month. It went faster and faster until it hurtled off the tracks. We reckon we'll jump off before it reaches Devil's Bend and then dig the gold out of the wreckage.'

Tucker and Clay both backed away for a pace to the rail. They looked down at the tracks speeding along below, then faced them while smirking.

'It's a good plan,' Nathan said, 'except Devil's Bend has a drop of several hundred feet. Nobody can get down there.'

Nathan firmed his jaw and kept still, hoping they wouldn't detect his lie. On the other side of the glass, Tucker shook his head.

'We've survived falling down the slope and being blown up. We're feeling lucky enough to risk it.' He folded his arms with a show of defiance while Clay edged to the side to peer around the side of the car. 'I hope you three feel lucky in there.'

Nathan turned away from the door and faced the other two.

'We've used up our luck,' Jeff said. 'So what can we do?'

'Exactly what we were doing before,' Nathan said. 'We break down the door.'

'But they're on the other side.'

'They are.' Nathan smiled. 'But they're not armed. They can't stop us.'

Jeff joined Nathan in smiling. Then he turned on his heel and strode down the aisle to the other door. He wasted no time in swinging back his arm and

136

using the rock to batter the side of the door.

Nathan stayed to watch Tucker's and Clay's reaction, and it was the one he'd expected. They glared through the glass at them, then Clay moved away.

A few moments later thudding sounded as Clay clambered on to the roof.

'Let's hope he falls off,' Patrick said.

Nathan left Patrick watching Tucker and joined Jeff, who was maintaining a steady rhythm battering the door. He gouged out a small hole. Splinters flew suggesting that if they had enough time, this tactic would work.

Nathan looked through the window then winced.

The slope was becoming more pronounced, as was the long sweep of the tracks, and two miles on that sweep took the tracks over a deep gorge through which the river ran. The approach tracked around the side of a steep-sided ridge with a sheer drop on one side before it slipped into a cutting that led on to the bridge over the deep gorge.

'Devil's Bend,' Nathan murmured.

Jeff broke off from hammering to look up through the window.

'It has to be,' he said before he restarted.

The footfalls on the roof had now stopped, but then again the car was rattling as it built up pace and Nathan wouldn't have been surprised if Clay had decided against clambering over it. He relayed this information to Jeff, encouraging him into delivering a huge swipe with the rock.

The strength of the blow made slithers of gold spray around, but the door cracked down the side from top to bottom and jerked out to come to a halt against the bar Clay and Tucker had put across. That didn't keep Jeff at bay for long – he put the rock down and kicked with the flat of his boot against the broken door.

Two kicks knocked the bar away and let the door fall over, giving them a full view of the scene ahead. The tracks were blurring towards them faster than Nathan had ever seen them do on any train ride and they were speeding up with every turn of the wheels as they hurtled on towards the cutting.

'We have to find a place to jump,' he said, beckoning Patrick to follow them.

Jeff nodded and with the nugget tucked under an arm he headed through the doorway to the rail. In a blur of motion Clay dropped down from the roof. He landed on Jeff's shoulders, knocking him forward into the rail before he slipped off him and to the floor.

The gold nugget came loose and went skittering along to slam against the railing. Everyone turned to watch its progress.

Clay was the first to get his wits about him. He leapt at the nugget, scooping it up in his arms, but that gave Jeff enough time to get to his knees and leap on his back.

He pushed him down, sending him to one knee hunched over the rock. Nathan moved into the doorway where he looked for an opening to help his friend, but Jeff had the upper hand.

Rapid footfalls sounded behind him. He expected them to be Patrick's and he half-turned while raising a hand, a comment that they had the situation under control on his lips.

Then he saw that Tucker was approaching. He had removed the bar from the other door and had come in, knocking Patrick over in his eagerness to join the fray.

Nathan swung round to take him on, but Tucker was too quick and pushed him back into the door-frame where he held him firmly. With his back braced, Nathan shoved forward, but he couldn't move Tucker away, and outside Clay was fighting back.

Clay raised himself, lifting Jeff off the floor sprawling over his back. Then, bent double over the rock, he side-stepped towards the rail, aiming to throw Jeff over the side.

'Give up, Jeff!' Nathan shouted. 'Let him have the gold.'

Jeff broke off from his attempts to push Clay down to look at the tracks. The ground to the left was falling away as they reached the sweeping approach to the cutting, then the bridge.

The car was travelling so fast the wheels were

screeching and the whole structure was shaking from side to side suggesting they might come off the tracks even before they reached Devil's Bend.

Worse, with the rock closing in to the right and the sheer drop to the left they couldn't leap off either. The only hope Nathan could see was that the cutting before the bridge would provide enough room for them to jump and roll aside.

With the urgency of the situation growing with every second, Jeff kicked up a foot and planted it on the rail to avoid being thrown over the side then swung his opponent round towards the door. Clay was still concentrating on holding the gold and so he went tumbling into Nathan, knocking him into the car and dragging Tucker with him.

Nathan moved to get up, but failed when the car skipped. It felt as if the car were tipping over before it slammed back down on the tracks.

All five men were now on their knees and struggling to raise themselves.

'We have to get off now,' Patrick shouted from behind them. 'Whoever lives gets the gold.'

This offer concentrated everyone's minds and with only the minimum of pushing, they all worked their way through the door. The shaking was too great to let any of them gain their feet and when Nathan emerged he saw that they were heading for the cutting.

They had almost reached the end of the section of

track with the sheer drop. If they could stay on the tracks for just a few more moments, they might have somewhere to jump to.

Tucker reached the rail first. He peered down at the drop to the side then looked to the cutting. He swirled round to Clay, the wind whipping his hat off and sending it flying around the side of the car.

'On three, jump,' he shouted, the wind that had taken his hat stealing his words away and making them emerge as a screech.

'We'll never make it,' Clay cried out, the weight of the nugget making it impossible for him to stand.

Tucker reached down to help him up, but by the time he'd dragged him to his feet it was too late. They'd hurtled into the cutting. Rocks blurred by on either side, preventing them from leaping off.

With the car creaking and groaning so loudly it could derail at any moment, Nathan grabbed the rail then walked himself up to a standing position. But that only brought him closer to Tucker, who risked releasing the rail to deliver a backhanded swipe at his head.

The hand caught him only a glancing blow, but with his grip of the rail being weak and with the wind buffeting him it was enough to send him spinning to the side rail.

He folded over the rail and the frightening sight of the ground hurtling by below confronted him. The rocky side of the cutting was only a few feet away.

141

He fought his way upright then tried to use the rocking of the car to swing himself back towards the door, but Tucker leapt at him.

The action bent him double. His feet left the base of the car and he headed towards the rock.

Over the rattling of the wheels, he heard Tucker utter a cry of triumph, but the shaking car that had made it hard for him to get to his feet rescued him. The car lurched heavily to the side, making it feel as if it were flying, and threw him backwards.

He slammed into Tucker sending him reeling into the front rail where he tipped over and disappeared from view beneath the car. Clay watched him go, hanging on with one hand on the rail and the other clutching the nugget.

While Patrick and Jeff fought to join him, Nathan looked ahead as the car emerged from the cutting like a bullet from a gun.

'We did it,' he shouted. 'We survived Devil's Bend.'

Patrick crawled to the railing and peered through.

'No we haven't,' he cried. 'That wasn't Devil's Bend.'

'What do you. . . ?' Nathan's question died on his lips.

The cutting had taken them to the side of the bridge. To swing down to it, the final quarter-mile stretch of tracks had a steep slope that only a train going at a careful speed could traverse.

They had to jump off now even if the speed at

which the ground was hurtling by said they'd never survive the fall. Nathan fought his way to the side rail. He felt as if he were trying to climb a sheer cliff face. Then he found that he was in fact doing that.

The car was tipping over.

The motion tore his grip away from the rail and sent him tumbling. His shoulder crashed against the door jamb. In desperation he grabbed hold of the wood and swung himself into the car, but whether or not that would turn out to be a good move he didn't know.

Unable to stop himself, he tumbled towards the side of the car, which became the base when the car crashed down its side. As he again went tumbling, he heard the others shouting, but over the screech of tortured metal and breaking wood he couldn't hear the words.

He rolled into a bench and he wrapped his arms around it, stilling his motion. He clung on with his teeth gritted as the grinding and screeching continued.

A plank landed on his back mashing his face against the bench and a massive jolt ripped through the car, but still he gripped the bench as if only it could save his life.

It felt as if the collapsing of the car would continue forever, but then with a grinding of timbers and a final tortured scream of metal, the car lurched to a halt.

143

He had an odd feeling of weightlessness and he wondered if the car had tipped over the side of the tracks and he was plummeting to the ground below. But all remained still.

He looked down and the disorientating sight of his legs sticking straight out confronted him. Seemingly they were suspended in the air. Then, with a sudden change of perspective, he saw that the car was lying on its side and he was holding on to a bench that had been bolted down to what was now effectively a wall.

With his arms beginning to ache, he dropped down to the base. The motion made him sway, although he had the impression that it was the car that swayed, not him. Then he looked for other survivors.

Jeff was sitting further down the car rubbing his head while Patrick was crawling away from him towards the door at the opposite end of the car.

Of Clay there was no sign, and neither could he see the gold nugget, but right now he reckoned he'd settle for just being alive. The door was beside him, now set sideways into the new wall.

He clambered over broken planks and benches then looked outside. He could see nothing but sky; he shook himself, still feeling disorientated, then looked down.

They had come to rest on the bridge. The long sweep of Devil's Bend was above. He breathed a sigh

144

of relief then turned to pass on the welcome news to the others.

A crack sounded, spraying splinters from the side of the door. He ducked while looking around, wondering if the car might still collapse, but then registered what the sound had been.

Someone had torn off a gunshot outside. He raised himself to look over the side of the door. A man was approaching.

Foley Steele was coming on to the bridge.

CHAPTER 14

'Foley's here,' Nathan said, turning back to look along the car.

'Foley?' Patrick said, pausing from his slow progress towards the opposite door. 'How did he get here?'

'I'd guess he worked out where we went too.'

'What happened to Clay?' Jeff said, getting to his feet.

'He wouldn't let go of the gold,' Patrick said, looking to the end of the car. 'But when he crashed into the door he tumbled out to his death. That made him let go.'

Patrick pointed to the corner and when Nathan moved to the side he saw the gleam of gold.

'Clay might have survived out there,' he said.

'He didn't,' Patrick said. He tentatively crawled on for another foot. 'And you two need to get back to the other end or we won't either.'

Nathan was about to ask what he meant, but then Foley spoke up from the other side of the doorway.

'Give me the gold,' he said, 'and I'll leave before you die in there.'

'No deal,' Jeff said before Nathan could retort.

'Then I'll wait until you're more amenable. It shouldn't be long.'

Foley laughed, making Nathan glance at Jeff quizzically, but he merely pointed to the far end of the car where Patrick was now five feet from the nugget. He was nervously edging forward an inch at a time even though there were no obstacles between him and the gold.

Nathan got to his feet to stand beside what had been the top of the door. He peered out at the bridge while still keeping out of Foley's sight.

The situation was worse than he'd feared.

The car had come to rest skewed across the tracks and from the amount of the bridge Nathan could see, he judged that around half of it was protruding over the edge. Patrick was now making his way across wood that was dangling over a two hundred-foot drop to the water below.

That journey became even more precarious when the car lurched. Patrick jerked back and the car settled, making him shuffle round to a sitting position and face them. He shook his head then held out his hands signifying he was some way short of reaching the nugget.

147

They might have been able to use the broken wood scattered around the car to drag the heavy nugget closer, but Nathan judged that they didn't have the time. The car was creaking so loudly it could fall even if they kept it balanced, and Foley's presence was making the situation even more fraught.

Nathan snorted a loud laugh then raised his voice.

'Hey, Foley,' he shouted. 'It's time we stopped working against each other.'

'I've given you my deal,' Foley said. 'You send the gold out and I'll leave you.'

'We can't do that. So I'm going to trust you. You'd better repay that trust or you'll never get the gold.'

Before Foley could reply Nathan stepped into the doorway with his hands raised. Foley was standing ten feet from the car, his gun drawn and aimed through the doorway.

'You don't tell me what to do,' he said. 'Now bring out the gold or I shoot.'

'If you shoot, I'll make sure I fall outside and then you'll never see the gold.'

Foley narrowed his eyes. 'What kind of threat is that?'

'It's a good one.' Nathan nodded back into the car. 'The gold is at the far end. We can't reach it unless we have more weight at this end. Your weight will do.'

'You expect me to believe that?' Foley snorted, although he did edge to the side to appraise the car.

'Believe what you will, but unless we co-operate none of us are getting the gold.'

Nathan and Jeff both folded their arms with a show of defiance and with neither man adding anything more Foley advanced a cautious pace towards the car. He craned his neck, trying to see in through the door. He must have noticed Patrick standing at the far end as he edged a pace closer and then on to the other side of the doorway.

He considered their predicament then snorted a hollow laugh.

'All those years of waiting,' he said, the anger gone from his voice, 'and it comes to this.'

He gestured for Nathan and Jeff to stand aside then clambered over the doorframe to join them. He stood back against the wall where he could keep everyone in view then motioned for Patrick to move on.

Patrick glared at him, looking as if he would refuse, but slowly he turned to the gold. He edged forward, this time not getting a complaint from the wrecked car.

In a hurry, as if speed would counteract the force of gravity, he lurched forward to the nugget. Using a deft motion that he must have mentally rehearsed he scooped it up in his arms then pranced backwards for two paces.

'Got it!' he said. He turned sporting a huge smile that slipped away when the reality of the situation

149

intruded upon his triumph.

'I'm pleased you've got my gold,' Foley said. 'Now bring it here and we can end this.'

'If you steal my gold,' Patrick said, 'you don't think it'll end here, do you?'

Foley shrugged. 'You'll come after me, I know, but I took your horses from the mine, so you'll be a while coming.'

'It took years the last time, and we can spend years again. You'll never get to enjoy it.' Patrick took two longs paces forward then kicked over a bench that had come loose, righting it. He placed the nugget on it then sat. 'But it doesn't have to end that way.'

Foley narrowed his eyes. 'What you planning?'

Patrick merely folded his arms and raised his chin in a show of not speaking.

Foley cast Jeff and Nathan stern glares that warned them not to try anything then paced through the debris to the bench. Nathan judged that Patrick had chosen a position where he could sit on what was effectively the edge of the bridge.

With a last glance around to check on where everyone was, Foley sat. Only then did Patrick speak up.

'It's time to do a deal,' he said. 'We split this four ways. That'll be enough for everyone.'

'You have nothing to bargain with, and I have a gun.'

'You do.' Patrick glanced over his shoulder at the nearest window, which now lacked glass and which, even from Nathan's position, provided a dizzying view down to the river below. 'And I have the gold. Make one wrong move and I throw it through the window.'

'You wouldn't throw it away.'

'If I can't have a share, I have nothing to lose.'

'Do that and I kill you.'

Patrick placed a hand on the top of the nugget.

'Then do it. As long as those two good men live, I won't mind. They may even manage to fish it out of the water.'

As Foley grunted with anger, at the back of the car Nathan glanced at Jeff, who nodded, acknowledging he was ready to take on Foley if Patrick's solution to the stand-off failed.

'Why do you care about them?' Foley asked.

'Because this situation is the same as the last time. I wanted to share the gold, but that wasn't good enough for you. You killed everyone and we all lost out. This time do the right thing.'

Foley firmed his shoulders, appearing as if he were mulling over the offer before he gave a slow shake of the head.

Patrick sighed then caught Nathan's eye with a darting glance that said the time for negotiation was over. Nathan had hoped they could avoid escalating the confrontation, but he accepted they now had no choice and he moved on with Jeff at his side.

He vaulted the debris before him and ran on, but

151

he'd managed only two paces when Foley swung up from the bench and turned to keep them all in view, his gun cocked and his finger on the trigger. But he stayed his fire.

Jeff and Nathan slid to a halt while Patrick took advantage of the delay to clutch the nugget to his chest and half-rise, putting himself in a position where he could swing round and tip it through the nearest window.

'That's far enough,' Foley muttered. He roved his gun back and forth taking in everyone. 'Give me the gold.'

Patrick considered him then the gold nugget. He shrugged.

'If you *insist*,' he said, only his rising tone on the last word hinting about what he'd planned. He hefted the nugget in his arms then hurled it at Foley.

Foley flinched away while raising a hand to ward off the rock, but then thought better of making the attempt and jumped to the side. Unfortunately he leapt away from Nathan and Jeff and that moved him towards the suspended section of the car.

Boards creaked ominously and the car wobbled, making everyone thrust out their arms for balance.

The gold hammered into the wall, then landed with a resounding crunch, breaking the boards beneath it and making the car creak again. Foley moved for the gold, but he'd weakened the boards beneath his feet and his right foot broke through, sending him to one knee.

In desperation he grabbed a bench, which toppled over, but it still stopped him slipping any further down. Jeff and Nathan moved towards him while Patrick went for the gold, but Foley got his wits about him and using his free hand he swung up the gun.

Everyone slid to a halt, surrounding him in a semi-circle. Despite his precarious situation, Foley grinned.

'Seems I'm nearest the gold,' he said. He gestured with his gun, ordering them to stand back.

Nathan saw that he had no choice and with Jeff he backed away for a pace, but Patrick didn't move. Instead he looked down through the nearest window then winced.

'Perhaps forever,' he said.

Foley continued to beam in triumph as Patrick caught Nathan's eye then glanced at the doorway. Nathan knew what he was suggesting, but after everything they'd been through, he couldn't do it.

'Complete your promise,' Foley muttered. 'This is your final warning.'

'I intend to,' Patrick said. 'Our feud ends here in the only way it ever could.'

Foley and Patrick glared at each other. Foley must have seen something in Patrick's eyes that warned him of his next action.

He fired. The shot blasted into Patrick's chest as he threw himself forward. Patrick still ran on for a pace and while folding over he ploughed into Foley, tearing his grip away from the bench.

Boards snapped and behind Nathan something heavy clattered to the floor making the car lurch. Despite Patrick's last order, he and Jeff still moved to help him, but the car continued to lurch and Nathan had the weird feeling of being unbalanced, making it hard to keep his footing.

Then he realized what was happening. Gravity had finally won the battle to keep the car in its precarious position. It was tipping over the side of the bridge.

Patrick had come to rest lying on his side clutching the gold while Foley tried ineffectually to free himself from the board that had trapped his leg. Patrick looked up at Nathan and winked. Then he flopped down, his dead weight rolling to the side to further hinder Foley's efforts to extricate himself.

'We have to get out now,' Jeff murmured with his arms outstretched as he struggled to keep his balance.

Nathan didn't need any more encouragement. He turned to the doorway, but it was ten feet away and already the car had tipped to such an angle he could manage only a pace towards it. Worse, he then slid backwards as the car embarked on its inevitable final journey.

Jeff lurched towards him. He grabbed his arm then tried to drag him towards the doorway, but he couldn't clamber up the rapidly rising base either.

Forlornly Nathan looked at Foley as he reached for the nugget as if that could somehow save him, but the sight of his ankle trapped in the floor gave Nathan an idea.

With no time to think it through, he gathered a mutual grasping of arms with Jeff. Then he turned away from the doorway. Jeff resisted at first, but the rising car tipped him towards Nathan and gave him no choice but to let Nathan direct him.

Both men took a staggered pace and then lost their footing in the rising car. They went sprawling on to the base amongst the benches and broken wood. But what was now the floor had once been the wall and Nathan rolled them towards a window. They fell through it and landed on the tracks as with some grace the car tipped away from them leaving them both lying on the bridge.

Nathan had a last glimpse of Foley struggling and Patrick lying still. As the car slipped over the side, he was sure he saw a flash of gold from the nugget embedded in the wall.

Then it fell from view, carrying Patrick and the gold away.

CHAPTER 15

'We'll never get down,' Nathan said. 'Leave it.'

Jeff moved from side to side still looking for a way down the near sheer side of the gully to the water below. But with a slap of a fist against his thigh he accepted that Nathan was right.

For the first hour after the demise of the car, they'd tramped up and down both sides of the gully, but they could find no way down. Even if they had been able to get down, the water was deep and the sides were so steep there wasn't even enough room to stand.

The car had landed on its side then floated fifty yards downriver where it'd caught on two protruding boulders. With the current battering against it, the car slowly broke up, releasing two bodies to the raging foam.

So with an acceptance that rescuing the gold would be even harder than they'd thought, for the

156

next hour they'd knocked ideas back and forth about what they could do if they had a rope and nerves of steel. Neither man felt enthused about the risk, even for the huge rock that was trapped inside the car.

The sun was lowering towards the horizon when even that possibility disappeared.

With a grinding of timbers the car succumbed to the pressure and snapped in two. Half of it went sailing down the river where it smashed into another boulder that broke it up further while the other half sank.

Later, fragments bobbed up further downriver.

'The gold nugget's at the bottom of the river,' Jeff said, summing up their problem again, as if that might help them find a solution.

'It's small enough to get moved by the water,' Nathan said, 'but large enough to take a while to fetch up somewhere.'

'So we could head downriver and find somewhere where the water is shallow then hope it rolls down to meet us.'

Nathan snorted at the likelihood of this wild idea working before he waved a dismissive hand at the river and stood up. Jeff joined him and the two men walked back towards the bridge.

With Foley having taken their horses from Copper Town, they were free to move on, if they were prepared to abandon the gold. But with both men having already resigned themselves to failure, when they paced on to the bridge, Nathan broached the real decision they had to make before dark.

'Back to Copper Town, or elsewhere?' he asked.

Jeff took one last look at the receding debris then swung round to look back along the rail tracks towards the mine.

'I never wanted to be a miner,' he said. 'What I saw back there hasn't changed my mind.'

'Agreed.'

'So I reckon we go back to Snake Pass and. . . .'

'And?' Nathan asked when Jeff didn't continue.

Jeff stood rigidly. Then he raised a hand bidding Nathan to stay back. With cautious steps he paced towards the section of the bridge where the car had toppled over. He dropped to one knee and scooped something up, then came back grinning.

He opened his hand to reveal the object on his palm. It was the size of Nathan's thumbnail and golden.

'It must have broken off when we were breaking through the door,' Jeff said.

Nathan grinned then joined Jeff in searching for more pieces. With the low sun casting glittering reflections off the pieces and making them stand out, they found several more, although the first piece remained the largest.

By the time darkness was descending, they'd gathered up a dozen small nodules of gold.

'How much do you reckon these are worth?'

158

Nathan asked, peering at their collection.

'I don't know, but it's sure to be enough for a few meals and a whiskey in Patrick's memory.' Jeff smiled. 'I'll settle for that.'

'I will too, and Patrick would be pleased to know we got some of his gold.'

Jeff considered for a moment then laughed.

'And if we really want to honour his memory, we can tell tales for whiskey about the huge gold nugget that got lost in the river.'

Nathan nodded and so, smiling, the two friends headed off the bridge to their mounts.

As they rode away from the river towards Snake Pass, Nathan looked up at the stars, as he had done on their first night of their mission to find the nugget.

This time he didn't imagine that every star was a speck of gold.